Southernmost Son

A Brody Wahl Adventure
The Bric Wahl Mystery Series
(Book seven)

Wayne Gales

For Tina, the love of my life

"Normal" is just a setting on your dryer

Everybody want to go to heaven
But nobody want to go now – Kenny Chesney

Wayne Gales

Forward

To paraphrase the late President Ronald Regan, "Well, here we go again." When I finished Southernmost Exposure, I was sure the Bric Wahl series was done, and as I approached my seventh decade, and a dozen years of writing, I was ready to take a break, produce a few books for other people and work on a couple of kids book ideas. After a few months, overwhelmingly positive reviews started coming in on *Southernmost Exposure*, and I began to realize how much readers enjoyed the stories and how disappointed they were to see the Bric series end. I kept getting messages and emails encouraging me to write again, so I turned to the logical solution, Brody. I said before that I wouldn't just put words in a row. The readers deserve more than that. A good mystery, a little adventure, a helping of smut, a touch of action, with a smattering of historical background, seems to be the formula, so here goes.

In the last book, I intentionally left out any mention of this Pandemic which has become the most significant event of my lifetime. My forefathers went through the birth of a country, the War of 1812, the civil war, the Spanish flu, World Wars One and Two, And Korea. I've lived through Viet Nam, 911, the recession of the '80s, the middle east conflicts, and more. It's a vain generation to think we would escape this life unscathed. I've lived constantly in fear that this year would be my last, the first time in my life since I was eleven years old when I spent days and nearly sleepless nights with the earpiece of a transistor radio in my ear, with the real fear that ballistic missiles, tipped with Russian nuclear warheads and only ninety miles from the U.S. coast, could lay waste to half my country at the push of a button.

People to recognize. The technical assistance from Bill Black continues to be priceless. Bill's the real deal. On more than one occasion I have texted a treasure-hunting question to Bill and he's answered, "Let me get back to you. We're over an eighteenth-century Spanish Galleon and I have divers in the water right now." Who else has that kind of expertise at hand? It's like having Albert Einstein at your beck and call to talk physics or being able to call

Steven Hawking to discuss black holes. I'm truly blessed. Thank you, Bill.

A special thank you to marine archeologist Dr. Lubos Kordac who lives in the Dominican Republic Dr. Kordac helped me with some technical aspects regarding Manila Galleon construction. He wrote Shipwrecks of the Dominican Republic among others.

Accuracy is always important. As always, I rely on my old airline buddy, Mark "Caretaker" Strussenberg for my correct depiction of period firearms. He reviewed the chapters involving guns and has caught more than one blunder. Thank you!

Thanks to my loving wife Tina, my rock, my love, my life, my best friend and relentless advocate when I had hospital time, and a capable nurse to a terrible patient when I came home. She has endured my struggles through early drafts throughout the years and always offers tasteful suggestions to my diatribes of drivel.

I dedicate this book to her.

Wayne Gales, April 2024

This is a re-write of book number seven. Touched up, re-edited, and cleaned up a little. It's partly because my publisher would not cancel the agreement per the contract. I don't have enough or make enough to hire a lawyer, so this edition is a classic end-run.

Enjoy.

Southernmost Son

Wayne Gales

1

For as long as I can remember, my dreams were dull, infrequent, and always in black and white, chasing some obscure fish with a speargun or boating that monster wahoo. And the vision that always plagues every young boy and girl, coming to school and realizing you forgot your pants, or worse yet, find yourself cuddled under your desk, naked and trying to hide before anybody notices. For that matter, most of the time, I forgot what I was dreaming about the moment I woke up. From what Dad told me, that's a huge departure from his dreams. He has told me many times, his dreams are manic, colorful, violent, erotic, and more than once, almost prophetic or visionary. No, my dreams were nothing like that.

Until now.

I was once told that a dream was a movie inside your head. You are the producer, director, in charge of special effects, casting, action, and location.

But you have absolutely no control of the plot.

I don't dream every night, but it seems when I do, it shows up eventually during the night and always makes me come awake with a jolt in a cold sweat. For the first time, I'm dreaming in color. Brilliant color, Technicolor. Before I only heard voices in my head, like mind reading, but now there are sounds, shouting, running, gunshots.

So real. So real.

I'm walking down a hall. There are doors on each side. The floor seems metallic and I have to walk softly to avoid noisy echoes. There's a feeling of danger, but I'm not sure who or what the danger is. I'm not alone, but can't see who is with me. There's a noise, a 'ka-thunk, ka-thunk' sound in the distance but I don't know where it's coming from. I walk down the hall, trying every door and they open to empty rooms.

After what seems like an eternity, I find a door that opens. The room isn't empty. It's a large room, with indistinguishable items on the wall, and a single chair in the middle of the room,

11

with one naked light bulb hanging above it. There's a person in the chair, slumped over, bloody, shirtless, and unconscious, his eyes nearly swollen shut. When we enter the room, the person in the chair looks up and cries "Son?"

It's my father.

Southernmost Son

Wayne Gales

2

I am my father's son.

I guess that doesn't mean much to you, but this statement means life to me. My father is Russell Bricklin "Bric" Wahl, a near legend in this neck of the woods. Ex-Navy SEAL, treasure hunter, treasure finder, musician, innkeeper, bar owner, and my best friend.

Dad has gone from rags to riches to rags more times than he cares to tell me about, mother than a healthy trust fund that hit my bank account when I turned twenty-five. He has 'died' more times than Cher has retired, dated, *and potentially impregnated* at least half the eligible *and sometimes ineligible* female population in Key West. Pop has had as much trouble with the law as he's had to keep his unit in his pants. He's lucky he has fathered only one surprise, my half-sister Mary Beth.

That he knows of.

Russell Bricklin Wahl and Broderick Russell Wahl, Bric and Brody, also known as Bric and Brody. Dad gets his first name from his mother's maiden name, the Bricklin part from a distant ancestor, and the Wahls come from Germans in Minnesota. Broderick was my great-grandfather on my mother's side, one Broderick Sawyer, a crook, a murderer, and a scoundrel. Mom's family are Bahamian Conchs and can trace their heritage back to before the Revolutionary War. They were a close-knit group of people, fleeing the new United States to the British-held Bahamas so they could stay loyal to mother England. They met their future spouses either in church or at a family reunion. A lot of Conch family trees look more like a phone pole than a tree. They say you can't identify a Conch murder victim; *everyone* has the same DNA and *nobody* has any dental records.

Yes, to say Bric's life has been pretty dynamic over the decades is an understatement. Years ago, while trying to protect his boss's property, he got stabbed and nearly killed. He left Key West in a bizarre motorized house on a barge once, then got arrested when he came back, accused of committing a murder he couldn't have committed. He saved the life of an old Navy chum once in a desert truck race and earned a concussion for the effort.

15

He recovered a cache of stolen uranium for the government in a crazy deep North Sea tech dive and nearly died of the bends in the process. Instead of taking time off to recover, he was allowed to take a multi-country European vacation while accompanied by a beautiful blonde, Russian-born government agent bodyguard, only to learn she was working for the other side. She tried several times to kill him and eventually learned the hard way that he was the wrong person to mess with.

Then there was the time he rescued a couple of dozen white slaves and got stabbed and shot for the effort. He renovated an ancient family residence a few years ago, turning it into a bed and breakfast, only to find it haunted by three ghosts, then saw it burn to the ground after a few years. He tried to rehabilitate a lady cat burglar and got shot three times by a mob hitman for thanks. He bought a bar and fell in love with an attractive English bartender, only to nearly get shot when she used him for bait to flush out a notorious international criminal. Oh, I forgot to mention the time a Haitian Coast Guard officer tried to steal our gold and watched his soldiers try to kill my fiancée, Mallory.

Let's just say that didn't end up well for that Coastie either.

As they say, no good deed goes unpunished.

Oh, along the way, there was a touch of good with the bad. Dad discovered millions in gold bars, thousands of old English gold coins, and uncounted Spanish doubloons. We've come a long way from living on a derelict houseboat in Florida Bay, wondering where our next meal was coming from. I traded my Big Wheel for a mask and speargun before I was ten and learned how to shoot our dinner out of necessity. Yes, I said 'is' not 'was'. Pop is alive and kicking, living on Geiger Key. After Rumpy passed, he bought that little cottage on Big Pine from Rumpy's brother, Blotto, and then gave it back to him shortly after. Between the loss of his friend and the attempt on his life, made living there impossible.

Old man, curmudgeon, fossil, hermit? I could call Pop that, but you had better not to his face. He probably can't straight-arm an anvil these days but he can still send you to a chiropractor, arrange a visit from the tooth fairy, or kill you in five different ways with just his hands and bare feet.

Me? I'm happy, domestically tamed, and stupid in love with the most amazing human I have ever met, living life and enjoying every minute.

I met Mallory Cohen and her brother, David on our Haiti treasure adventure, diving on the *Never on Saturday*, a luxury yacht owned by her grandparents, Moishe and Golda. My dad worked for Moishe years ago when he was a starving diver, salvaging cannons, anchors, and other stuff from ancient wrecks and selling them to gas stations and souvenir stands. Mallory and David were born in America and raised in Israel. My dad was good friends with their father, Michael and he taught him how to scuba dive for treasure. Mal and David's parents sadly were killed by a suicide bomber in Israel long ago. Moishe and Golda adopted their grandchildren, Mallory and David, placing both in an Israeli Kibbutz while they grew up. David went on to earn several degrees and knows about everything related to Spanish treasure. His hair is short and so is his temper. He wears pop bottle glasses and looks more like an account than a treasure seeker. I learned that looks can be deceiving.

Mallory served two years in the Israeli Military and several years with Mossad, doing things she doesn't talk about much, other than becoming an accomplished diver. After recovering from a near-fatal shot from a Palestinian sniper, she got a Master's degree at the University of Israel. Now she is working on a doctorate at Cambridge University in England. Smart, beautiful, tough as nails, and has the cutest accent. I think she could make Chuck Norris laugh and cry at the same time. He would laugh when she told him she could kick his ass. Then she would kick his ass. I'm glad Mal and Dad are on the same side. If they ever tangled, it would be ugly. I think of her as having the face of an angel, the body of Christina Aguilera, and the mind of Mr. Spock.

I won't say it was love at first sight when I first saw her at the outdoor grill in Jamaica.

It took at least thirty seconds.

It wasn't like Mallory and I was going to do nothing for the rest of our lives. I have a decent trust fund in the bank, plus my share of the bounty from our adventures aboard the *Never on Saturday*, and I would guess Mallory was in line for a substantial inheritance from her grandparents someday. Just consider it a break between projects. There was no doubt David could call at any moment with another exciting, and possibly dangerous, adventure, but in the meantime, life was for living.

One morning, Mal rousted me out of bed at o-dark thirty. "Put your running gear on. It's time to work off a little of that baby fat!" I drug my ass out of bed, half-awake, dressed, stumbled out the door behind her and down the dock of our houseboat. I tried to keep up while we circled the island, up Roosevelt, down the other side, around the airport, West Martello, past White Street Pier, the East Martello, Casa Marina, and Southernmost Point before we turned up Duval Street. As we cruised past the bars, all still blissfully closed, I almost regretted my aversion to beer. We finally bent right on Truman for the final leg to the houseboat.

She almost had to carry me the last half mile.

While I sat on the floor of the house, chugging Gatorade and trying to wash the snow out of my vision, Mal reached for my hand. Expecting a high five for surviving the run, despite our substantial weight differential, she jerked me to my feet like a Raggedy Andy doll. "Get up! It's time you learned how to defend yourself."

"Remember, I'm a third-degree black belt in Tai-Wan-Do." I reminded her, with a sniff.

"And I have no doubt there's not a pine board in Florida that's safe around your feet, should an attacker hold it still in front of you," she countered. "But I've seen you 'defend' yourself. On a good day, you couldn't fight your way out of a wet paper bag."

She went on to remind me. "When I met your dad, I told him I had six years with Mossad where I learned to dive, among other things. It's time you learned what those 'other things' were." Mal continued, "We both found out the hard way a few months ago, first hand that this world can be a violent place. I think your father has left more than one skeleton in the closet. Despite promises from some mutual friends, I suspect his dance isn't done. It's time you learn the best self-defense is a good offense."

We cleared the furniture out of the houseboat living room. That morning, and for the next several weeks, I had some stern lessons in 'other things'. I would describe Mallory's hand-to-hand combat skills as a cross between a bobcat, a wolverine, and a rabid

Tasmanian Devil. She was a patient, but persistent coach. We started with a five-mile run each morning, and then we would go through what she called 'defensive training' and I called, 'getting the crap beat out of me'. After six weeks of what she considered gentle persuasion, I started to consider adding a hot tub to the porch. She was more of a Mohamed Ali to my Smokin Joe Frasier, but she adjusted and honed my skills daily. I'll never be the fighting machine my father was, I think I could hold my own in a pinch. I will never match her combat skills but after a month of running, I could push her pace, finally passing her on the last leg to home one morning. Eventually, the bruises faded from the color of a baboon's ass to a dully yellow.

You would think after being brutalized all day, the nights would be peaceful, but Mal had other ideas. We spent at least a half dozen hours four nights a week in 'Charm School'. Proper English was hammered into my head, she pounded the redneck country boy out of my language, my cursive became halfway legible and I began to understand there was life beyond cargo shorts, a camouflage rash guard shirt, and purple size eleven Crocks. Whoda thunk that I would learn proper English from an American raised in Israel? Go figure.

I didn't throw away those Crocks.

Married? Not yet. Soon, someday. I still had that ring that Dad gave me, I know precisely where I left it, stuffed at the end of an athletic sock, on a box, in a drawer, in a dresser. In a storage unit. I knew where to find it when the time was right. No rush. This was a commitment that didn't require a piece of paper. Or a minister, a rabbi, or for that matter a witch doctor with a long beard in flowing robes standing on top of an active volcano swinging a dead possum on a string.

Everything was going just ducky.

Until it wasn't.

3
Flashback

The Manila Galleon was the commercial route that existed from 1565 to 1815 between Asia and America through the Pacific Ocean. It connected the main ports of Manila and Acapulco. The Manila Galleon Trade Route was a key part of the American-European trade, fostered by the Spanish Crown. Which consisted of taking advantage of its imperial territories for the acquisition of highly appreciated East Asian goods. This was an alternative to the long and dangerous land routes through Central Asia and the one that surrounded Africa by ship, a route that was monopolized by Portugal.

The Manila Galleon was a result of the advances in maritime technology. To begin with, Spaniards had an advantage in their knowledge of the Pacific Rim. The trips of Magellan, Lopez de Legazpi, and de Urdaneta offered viable routes to connect America and the Philippines to Spain, and the capacity of the Spanish ships increased significantly during this period. To compare, *La Santa Maria*, the largest ship of the first Columbus trip to America in 1492, was about fifty feet long and could carry forty people, while *La Concepcion*, one of the ships used in the Manila Galleon in the seventeenth century was 150 feet long, with a burden of about 2,000 tons, and the capacity to carry a crew between 300 and 500 people.

Perhaps the most valuable, if not the largest cargo on the galleons, was the exotic spices from the famed Spice Islands. Today, these islands are no longer known as "The Spice Islands," recognized now as the Moluccas. They are made up of an Indonesian archipelago that comprises a total landmass of nearly three thousand square miles. The Moluccas have been inhabited for tens of thousands of years and the spice trade was conducted by the native people long before the first Europeans set foot on the islands.

Wayne Gales

Spices, such as cinnamon, cassia, cardamom, ginger, pepper, and turmeric were known and used in antiquity for commerce in the Eastern World. These spices found their way into the Near East before the beginning of the Christian Era, where the true sources of these spices were protected by the traders and associated with fantastic tales.

The maritime aspect of the trade was dominated by the people in Southeast Asia who established the trade routes from Southeast Asia to Sri Lanka and India by at least 1500 BC. These goods were then transported by land further on towards the Mediterranean and the Greco-Roman world via the Incense Route and the routes established by India and Persian traders. The maritime trade lanes later expanded into the Middle East and eastern Africa by the 1st millennium AD, resulting in the colonization of Madagascar.

Arab traders eventually took over conveying goods to Europe until the route was cut by Seljuk Turks in 1090 and the Ottoman Turks in 1453. Overland routes helped the spice trade initially, but maritime trade routes led to tremendous growth in commercial activities. During medieval periods, Muslim traders dominated maritime spice trading routes throughout the Indian Ocean, tapping source regions in East Asia and shipping spices from trading emporiums in India westward to the Persian Gulf and the Red Sea, from which overland routes led to Europe.

The trade was changed by the Crusades and later the European Age of Discovery, during which the spice trade, particularly in black pepper, became an influential activity for European traders. The Cape Route from Europe to the Indian Ocean via the Cape of Good Hope was pioneered by the Portuguese explorer and navigator Vasco da Gama in 1498, resulting in new maritime routes for trade.

This trade, which drove the world economy from the end of the Middle Ages well into the Renaissance, ushered in an age of European domination in the East. Channels, such as the Bay of Bengal, served as bridges for cultural and commercial exchanges between diverse cultures as nations struggled to gain control of the trade along the many spice routes. In 1571, the Spanish opened the first transpacific route between its territories of the

Philippines and Mexico, known as the Manila Galleon which lasted until 1815. The Portuguese trade routes were mainly restricted and limited by the use of ancient routes, ports, and nations that were difficult to dominate. The Dutch were later able to bypass many of these problems by pioneering a direct ocean route from the Cape of Good Hope to the Sunda Strait in Indonesia

In the 16th century, the Moluccas were nicknamed the "Spice Islands." This was due to the large number of aromatic plants that grew on this archipelago. Subsequently, the islands were an important strategic base for the highly profitable spice trade. Nutmeg and cloves largely drove the spice trade. These two widely-used spices were originally only native to this group of islands. Since spices were once worth their weight in gold, control of the Moluccas was synonymous with extreme wealth. The fight to take control of this "spice monopoly" flared up between Europeans until it became a major issue in 1512. After Vasco da Gama discovered a sea route to India, it wasn't long before other expeditions made their way further east and discovered the archipelago.

The Portuguese established several bases on the Spice Islands in 1512. Soon a bidding war started between the British, Dutch, Spanish, and Portuguese for control of the islands. After many clashes, the Dutch emerged victorious in 1663. The Dutch East India Company was then in control of the spice monopoly. They were the only ones who could deliver nutmeg or cloves and also had control over the price. Ironically, the Spice Islands were the reason for the first circumnavigation of the world. The Portuguese explorer Ferdinand Magellan wanted to find the first western route to the Spice Islands for the glory of Spain. Magellan's crew sailed around the globe, going first around the tip of South America and then on to the Philippines and the southern coast of Africa before finally heading back to Spain. Magellan himself died on the journey in armed conflicts with natives. The value that spices had then could be quantified with these facts: of the five ships that launched with Magellan, only one returned to Spain three years later. It was loaded with 26 tons of spices. After

Wayne Gales

deducting the cost of the lost ships, etc. a net profit of 500 gold ducats still remained.

The trade route consisted of at least, two phases. In the first phase, was *Carrera de Indias*, which was under the monopoly of Spanish merchants in Seville. It encompassed all the trade between Spain and its American colonies. The *West Indies Fleet* was the main element of Carrera de Indias. Second, there was *Carrera de Islas Poniente*, of a smaller scale in terms of the number and tonnage of the ships, as well as the volume and value of the exchanges. It was based on the Acapulco-Manila connection. Carrera de Islas Poniente was carried out, mainly, by merchants from Mexico City and Manila. Trade was regular, going practically uninterrupted for 250 years.

In preparation for the voyage to China, merchants gathered goods from several different origins. Acapulco loaded silver, cochineal for dyes, seeds, sweet potato, tobacco, chickpea, chocolate and cocoa, watermelon, vines, barrels of wine and fig trees. Olive oil from Spain, and swords, daggers, garrisons, knobs, and spurs from Germany, France, and Italy. The European goods arrived from Seville to Veracruz on the East Coast of Mexico and were transported by land to Acapulco. The composition of the cargo was fairly stable, being about eighty percent of the goods from America and twenty percent European. The cargo from Manila was more varied due to the smaller size of the American market. Most of the time, the cargo included goods from all over Asia. From China, jade, beeswax, gunpowder, silk fabrics, and other cloth products including stockings, handkerchiefs, bedspreads, and tablecloths. From the Middle East, rugs and camel wool. From India came cotton and amber. From Japan, fans, drawers, chests, folding screens, scribes, and porcelain. And from South East Asia, spices, mainly cloves, pepper, cinnamon, and nutmeg.

The Manila Galleon was a specialized international exchange, mainly of an inter-industrial nature. This is similar to the pattern predicted by the classic models of international trade, in which countries specialize in the activities in which they have comparative advantages. Additionally, the protectionist policies in place at the moment made it almost impossible for "non-exotic" imports to compete in the markets with domestic products.

Despite the independence of *Carrera de Indias* and *Carrera de Islas Ponientes*, the Spanish Crown was a synchronizing institution between them. The Crown established a strict regulation over the trade activity, limiting the number of merchants allowed to participate, defining the timing of the voyages, and restricting their routes.

Departing from Acapulco, the voyage required the crossing of a fairly uncharted ocean for at least four months per trip. Only two ships a year were allowed to sail. The cargo of these ships could not exceed 300 tons of weight, but smuggling illicit, undocumented cargo, was a regular activity in this trade route.

History shows that not every ship had a successful voyage. No less than forty ships were lost to storms, reefs, and overloading. Many more were captured or sunk by vessels of Spain's enemies, including the English, Portuguese, and Dutch.

After leaving the port of Cavite on Manila Bay, usually in July, a Manila Galleon would have to thread its way through the many islands and reefs and then head to the northern latitudes near Japan, then east toward the Americas. Eventually, they would come into sight of Cape Mendocino or nearby, off the northern California coast, and follow this coastline south to Acapulco. Many Manila Galleons were lost along this coastline.

Only a few have been found so far. These include:

Santa Marta - Ran aground on Santa Catalina Island off the California coast in 1528.

San Martin - Wrecked near Canton, China in 1578, with much silver on board. Two more vessels were also lost near Canton in 1598.

San Francisco - Wrecked off Japan in 1608, with a large amount of gold and silver.

Santissima Trinidad - Left Manila in 1616 with a cargo valued at over 3,000,000 pesos. A typhoon hit and she wrecked near the southern end of Japan.

Jesus Maria and the *Santa Ana* - Both these vessels sank in the San Bernardino Strait with over 2,000,000 silver pesos, after doing battle with a superior Dutch fleet, who ambushed them there in 1620.

The *Nuestra Señora de la Concepcion* - From Manila bound for Acapulco, she wrecked near the island of Saipan, in 1638. She was the largest Spanish vessel built up to this time, displacing about 2,000 tons.

San Diego - This wreck was found in Manila Bay in 1991. It is presently being excavated by divers and has yielded over 28,000 items to date.

Several yet undiscovered wrecks also lie off the California and Mexican coast.

San Ambrosio and another ship - Coming from Acapulco, both vessels were lost during a typhoon on the coast of Cagayan in 1639, with an estimated 2,000,000 silver pesos.

Nuestra Señora *de Ayuda* - Wrecked on a rock, west of Catalina Island in 1641.

Santa Maria de Los Valles - Left Manila in 1668 with 778 people and very valuable cargo. She arrived at Acapulco two days before Christmas and dropped anchor. Two hours later she caught fire and sank within an hour, taking with her all the treasure valued at over 3,000,000 pesos and more than 330 people.

Nuestra Señora *del Pilar* - Wrecked in 1690 near Guam.

San Agustin - Wrecked in Drake's Bay north of San Francisco, in 1690, and now lies in a part of the Point Reyes National Seashore Park.

Most of the Manila Galleons that sank were near the coast of the Philippines and along the trade route, including China and Japan.

Santo Cristo de Burgos - She grounded offshore of Ticao Island, Philippines, in 1726. Another vessel, the *San Andres*, wrecked on Naranjos Shoals near Ticao, October 1797.

Santa Maria Madalena - Crammed with so much cargo as to make her unsafe, she left Cavite in 1734, and capsized and sank within a few hundred yards of her anchorage.

San Sebastian - attacked by an English pirate in 1754, she was run aground just west of Santa Catalina Island.

These wrecks were some of the most valuable in the world at that time. While much documentation has been recorded regarding ships from the Far East, perhaps as many, or more were lost leaving the Americas on the return voyage, but only a few have been found. There could be as much, or more, treasure lying at the bottom of the Pacific as the fabulous treasure in the Caribbean, and there's far more treasure undiscovered in the Caribbean that has yet to be found.

Once in Acapulco, a small portion of the Asian cargo stayed in America, with part staying in present-day Mexico and the rest often via smuggling, to other parts of Spanish America. Much of the remaining Asian goods were sent to Peru, where aristocratic families demanded exotic goods and a considerable fraction ended up in more distant markets, such as Buenos Aires. The remaining products were taken to Veracruz by mule and then shipped to Seville, Spain.

The ancient trade routes through Asia were highly constrained by Islamic empires including the Ottomans, Safavid, and Mongolians, who were in control of the Middle East. The hostilities between these empires and Christian Europe were at a high peak. Meanwhile, in Europe, the Italian city-states played an essential role in Mediterranean trade for centuries.

The remaining Asian goods that ended in Europe were relatively small when compared to the total onboard. As much as ninety percent of the cargo departing from America towards Spain was gold and silver.

The share of the Asian cargo that remained in America was mostly sold at the Acapulco Fair. Merchants from different regions of New Spain participated with small amounts of money compared with those coming from Mexico City. The large merchants from Mexico City, every year spent several millions of pesos for purchases at the fair. This gave them the power to impose prices and, more importantly, to control the contracts and the regulation of the trade with Manila.

Part of the business that the Mexico City merchants controlled was the provision of goods to the government of Manila. The Spanish Crown had to support its presence in the Philippines, including administrative staff, military, and priests. Most of the management of the Manila Government was coordinated from New Spain, and the Crown. The New Spain Government established a contractual system that used the private sector to supply food and other goods to the Philippine Government. Mexico City merchants were constrained by the interests of European merchants.

In Manila, most of the commercial business was controlled by the Chinese. Chinese merchants had settled in Manila several decades before the arrival of Spaniards and were already connected to the most important commercial networks of the region. This community had a population that performed more than sixty different occupations. It included artisans, manufacturers, service providers, and vendors of all kinds. A large fraction of these activities intended to satisfy the demand for Asian goods from American and European markets.

The last voyage of the Manila Galleon took place in 1815.

Southernmost Son

Wayne Gales

4

Then we received that message from David on the *Never on Saturday*. The adventure sounded like fun. Untouched treasure off the coast of Mexico? Count me in. Since Bric's cell phone spent most of its time turned off, sitting in a bedside nightstand drawer, the message came to me on my phone. At the time, we were only a few miles south of Sand Key Light out in the gulf.

When I read the message, I was all in for spinning the *Seaglass* around right then and heading east for the Panama Canal. An untouched eighteenth-century Spanish Galleon in forty feet of water? It sounded too good after that Haiti adventure.

"Dad, let's go!" I said. "We can buy supplies in Panama or someplace on the way."

"Hold your horses," he cautioned. "Did it occur to you that not everyone on board this tub may be quite as enthusiastic about sailing off into the sunset for three or four months as you are? Besides," he added, "I need to pack a few things, like a spare tee-shirt, a toothbrush, and an extra hat, not to mention a spare gallon or two of Code Rum and some boat drink mix. That stuff doesn't exactly grow on trees in Mexico and tequila makes my tummy burn."

"And makes your clothes fall off," I added. "Okay," I conceded. "Back to the Rock, dump out any unwilling passengers, get some grub, and hit the high seas!"

As it turned out, dad was more than right about our little crew. The two deckhands, Becky and Brenda had college in the fall and couldn't come along. That left my father, Mal, and me to run this bucket along with the cook. I had resigned to never being able to pronounce his name, Wang Fang something, so I just called him Cookie. It wouldn't be impossible to sail the *Seaglass*, our 155 foot, three-masted ketch, with that size crew; she almost sailed herself, but there wouldn't be a lot of downtime on the trip. I think David expected us to climb on a plane and jet our way to Acapulco, but the thought of cramming ourselves and our dive gear into a metal tube for six hours didn't exactly melt my butter.

Wayne Gales

In my excitement, I hardly noticed Mallory standing there with her arms folded, looking sad and uncomfortable. Putting my arm around her waist, I asked. "Why so glum? Life's an adventure and we have a new one."

Her answer was so quiet I almost had to put my ear to her lips. "Brody, classes at the university are starting in three weeks. I'll need to leave the U.S. in a few days, a week at most. I'm so close to my doctorate, I can't quit now." Her head turned down. "I'm so sorry, Brody."

That was the last news I expected to hear. I was so excited about treasure hunting, I had completely spaced her education. Trying not to show my disappointment, I picked her up by the waist and twirled her around. "Then we better have a proper send-off before we get back to Key West!" Taking Mal by the hand, I led her below decks for some 'us' time. Let's just say I did all possible to put a bun in that oven before we parted so she would come home soon but wasn't successful.

That time.

With Mallory leaving, my vision of pulling up to the dock, throwing the girls off, and sailing west changed a little. Now I was all for spending a week onshore, or as long as I could before Mal had to go. When we got to port, I was surprised to find dad also suddenly had a change of heart. He wanted to sail *now*.

Saying a few quiet words to the girls before they walked up the dock, he turned back to us. "Let's top off the fuel, fill the potable water, dump the head, and sail." He said all this with a quiet voice, almost a stage whisper. And then I noticed what made him so nervous. He was watching a couple of ugly-looking characters that were standing on the shore near the ship's store. "Don't we need a few consumables before we head out for who knows how long?" I asked, still wanting to stretch our shore time.

"We can stop on the way as you suggested earlier. We have a good supply of dry goods stored on board." His answer was almost cryptic while he still kept a sideways glance on the dock. Mal caught his energy and turned to both of us. "I'm going to head up to the store, get you a few snacks and beverages, and tell the clerk that you only needed a few things to tide you over for a sunset sail."

"What did you say to the girls?" I queried.

"I apologized for such a casual sendoff since they are almost part of the family," Dad answered. "I also asked them to keep our destination to themselves. And, I promised that we would throw a proper going-away shindig in the future when we got back."

After bringing our drinks and snacks, Mallory sort of stood there, not wanting to leave. I took both of her hands in mine and muttered, "I guess this is goodbye, for now."

"Nonsense!" she answered. "Safe trip, au revior, bon voyage, but never goodbye." Mal took me by the hand and led me to the other side of the cabin. Once out of sight, she gave me a bear hug and a send-off kiss that I won't soon forget.

She didn't quite crack a rib.

Holding me close, she said quietly, "Take care of you, Brody, and don't have too much fun without me." She whispered in my ear, "Don't kiss any strange girls more than once." Holding me at arm's length she smiled sweetly, and added, "Remember, I can still beat the hell out of you. Give my best to my brother. I miss him dearly. And don't forget to bring home a little treasure."

With that, she turned and walked off the ship. Turning, as she walked away, she called back to us in a convincing voice, "Have a fun afternoon! I'll see you guys after dark!"

Fuel and water topped off, a normal activity even for a short cruise, dad backed *Seaglass* out of the mole. "This tub almost sails itself," he pointed out, "but we've been left a little thin on crew. I would have loved rounding up a few new deckhands, but it's not the right time to announce our destination to the world." He smiled at me. "Even on autopilot, we'll turn twelve on, twelve off until we get to Acapulco and meet up with the *Saturday*. It's nothing we can't live through."

"Where will we get supplies?" I asked.

"Well, we could hit Belize or Panama City, but I'd rather shop in the good old USA. Texas is a small detour. Brody, here's your chance to work on your navigation skills. Plot a course for Galveston." Checking the computer on the bridge for a moment, he added, "I show it's 871 miles." He started punching in numbers on the keyboard.

Looking at the clouds for an answer, like my dad always did, I answered. "If we can make sixteen knots, at 871 miles, that means we can get to Galveston in fifty-four point four hours. Call it two and a half days."

"How can you do that in your head quicker than I can punch it up on a computer?" Dad asked. "Normally I can't get you to make correct change for a dollar."

"Only if it's your dollar," I reminded him with a smile. "Numbers that mean something just show up in my head, like dive times," I answered, smugly.

As we pulled away, I looked up at the dock, concerned, "Won't those bad guys, if they *are* bad guys, get a little curious when we don't come home tonight?"

"By the time anyone figures out they have been end-runned, we'll be west of the Dry Tortugas," he answered. Stretching his arms wide, he added, "It's a big ocean out there. If somebody came looking, they wouldn't know which way to start."

We sailed all afternoon and into the evening. Wouldn't you know it, just as we passed the Marquesas, the gulf went glassy-calm and flat as a board, not exactly perfect weather for a sailboat. "It's a good thing the *Seaglass* is a motorsailer," Dad remarked. "Most sailboats just have a little donkey motor to get you around a harbor at two knots. I'm glad she has a couple of Paxman Diesels under her. We can't hold a candle to the *Saturday*, but we can push it to twenty-one knots in a pinch, and cruise comfortably at sixteen."

It had been a long day. "Skipper, take her helm," dad said, stretching. "I'm going below for a nap."

We made Galveston in the morning of day three, pulling up to an open slip in the marina. We topped off with diesel and caught a cab to the local Wal-Mart, stocking up on steaks, chicken, fruits, and vegetables, water and sodas for me, (sugar-free, of course,) and alcohol for Dad.

"The Panama Canal is over fourteen hundred nautical miles," I said, consulting my phone. "Looking at the forecast, we can make around eleven knots under sail. That's five and a half days, give or take a day. Best we stay under sail and save fuel for times of need."

"I concur, Captain Brody." Dad saluted smartly. "Take her out."

We accomplished the leg to Panama in a little more than a week. Sailing at that leisurely pace had the advantage of giving us the perfect trolling speed. We always drug some heavy line behind us with a bungee cord for a shock absorber and a leader with a couple of feathered jigs attached. Despite jumping the occasional sailfish or marlin, which we horsed in and released, we hooked enough mahi, wahoo, and even the stray cobia to supplement our diet. We arrived in Colon on the eastern or gulf side of the canal with more food than we left Galveston with, and not a drop of fuel used.

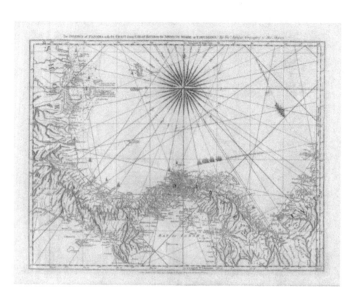

5
Flashback – Panama

Panama's strategic location, between two continents, has been a global crossroads ever since humans first passed through the country.

Previous research gauged that the earliest evidence of humans in South America was 12,500 years old but recent studies show humans may have settled in the Americas much earlier than previously thought, according to new finds from Mexico. They suggest people were living there as much as 33,000 years ago, twice the widely accepted age for the earliest settlement of the Americas.

Based on work at Chiquihuite Cave, a high-altitude rock shelter in central Mexico, archaeologists found nearly 2,000 stone tools, suggesting the cave was used by people for at least 20,000 years. That means that they may have passed through Panama shortly after that, as long as 25,000 years ago, although spearheads found in Panama date back only about 11,000 years ago, making them the first solid evidence of humans in the area.

Panama was too far south for Mayan and Aztec influence, and the thick jungles prevented much influence by the Andean civilizations to the south, and the indigenous peoples that the Spanish found were thus generally more primitive. They lived in small villages or survived as hunter-gatherers and fishermen. Indeed, the name "Panama" itself comes from an old native word meaning "abundance of fish."

Despite the lack of influence from the larger pre-Columbian civilizations, Panama's original residents were not fully-isolated. The region then, as now, was still part of a great Pan-American trading route. Gold, ornaments, and pottery have been unearthed from all over the Americas in Panama.

The first European to arrive in Panama was the explorer and conquistador Rodrigo de Bastidas. He first arrived in the New World with Columbus on his second voyage. After returning home from that voyage, Bastidas received permission to launch his own expedition. He set sail in 1499. After exploring the coast of northern Colombia, Bastidas reached Panama in 1501.

Although Columbus never reached or even saw what is now North America, he reached Panama in 1502, following the coast from Costa Rica in his fourth and final voyage. He put into shore in the Bocas del Toro, where the bay and a local town, Almirante, are still named after him. Columbus followed the coast along the top of Panama to what is now known as Portobelo, which he also named.

A few years later, in 1510, a full settlement of conquistadores arrived in the region. They founded a settlement called Santa Maria de la Antigua del Darien, which is now in modern-day Colombia. Santa Maria was the first European settlement on the American mainland and a base for all future colonization.

The leader of the settlers, Vasco de Nuñez de Balboa, first came to Panama with Bastidas in 1501. Balboa had his own ambitions for glory. He had heard from the indigenous people that there was another ocean close by and that the land he had settled was, in fact, an isthmus.

After crossing the isthmus and both conquering and befriending tribes along the way, Balboa finally walked into the Pacific Ocean as the first European to do so, in 1513. He claimed the whole sea for the Spanish Crown. It took another six years for the Spanish to begin colonizing the Pacific side of Panama.

In 1519, Pedro Arias Davila arrived in Santa Maria on the orders of the Crown to govern the area. The first thing he did was abandon the settlement and move across the isthmus to the Pacific. There, he founded a settlement called Nuestra Señora de la Asunción de Panamá, now known as Panama City. Using this settlement as a base, Davila built ships for the Pacific Ocean and sent explorers up and down the coast. The Pacific base for the Spanish ensured not only the conquest of Central America but also devastated the Inca Empire in Peru.

Once the Spanish had firm possession of the Americas, Panama became what it is today, a transit point for people traveling from one part of the world to another. Panama City also became the point where a lot of plundered treasure from the conquest of the Incas ended up before being shipped to Spain. As a result, the settlement became a town and the town became a rich city.

The Panama City that was founded by Davila lies about three miles east of present-day Panama City. The English pirate Henry Morgan burned Davila's original city to the ground in 1671. Being attacked by pirates was an occupational hazard of being a wealthy city that transported gold in the 17th century. Unlike the rest of Central America, Panama was part of the Viceroyalty of Peru. This meant that it took its orders from Lima instead of from Mexico or Guatemala City.

This crucial difference is still evident today. Panamanians don't see themselves as Central Americans or share Central American pride like the other countries on the isthmus. They have a different history.

The Viceroyalty of Peru got broken up into more manageable parts in 1717, as part of a restructuring exercise. Panama found itself part of the newly-formed Viceroyalty of New Granada. This new viceroyalty consisted of Venezuela, Colombia, and Ecuador, and was ruled from the Colombian city of Bogota.

The 1800s brought independence to most of Latin America as the Spanish Empire crumbled. President Theodore Roosevelt oversaw the realization of a long-term United States goal—a trans-isthmian canal. Throughout the 1800s, American and British leaders and businessmen wanted to ship goods quickly and cheaply between the Atlantic and Pacific coasts. In 1850, the United States and Great Britain negotiated the Clayton-Bulwer Treaty to rein in rivalry over a proposed canal through the Central American Republic of Nicaragua.

The contested stretch of land had a brief, but historical influx of travelers during the California gold rush. The Panama shortcut was an attractive way to get from the east to the west, cutting some eight thousand miles of travel off the treacherous sea voyage around Cape Horn, at the tip of South America. Worse yet was the overland route via wagon or on foot, in danger of Native Americans committed to protecting their land, across the vast plains and desert of the west. The trip through the jungles of Panama, with their brightly-colored birds and flowers, seemed at first to be an exotic adventure.

In 1849, Panama became popular and important to America when gold was discovered in California. Would-be gold seekers, dubbed forty-niners, had three ways to get from the East Coast to the West. They could take an arduous cross-country trip, either by wagon or foot, through mountains, deserts, and plains, with the threat of hostile Indians along the way, by ship via storm-ridden Cape Horn, or via the Isthmus of Panama, the shortest route but far from risk-free. The trip would start from the East Coast via ship to the Caribbean coast of Panama, where the cross-country journey began at the mouth of the Chagres River. There, forty-niners stepped on board a canoe, called a *bungoe* by the natives. At first, the natives charged about five dollars for the four-day river journey. But when they realized how anxious the gold seekers were to get across Panama, the price quickly rose. As the gold seekers traveled, they saw a jungle landscape that seemed like something from a dream: dense thickets of mangrove trees, dazzling tropical flowers, and exotic animals including crocodiles, parrots, and jaguars.

The forty-niners learned to bring bags of dimes with them. The Pillar dollar, commonly known as a piece of eight, was worth eight reals and traded on par with the U.S. dollar. When the real was cut into eight segments, each segment was known as a 'bit'. The American dime was also considered a bit, making eight dimes worth a dollar.

The river journey was the easy part. When the bungoes landed, men set out on horses or mules into the steaming jungle on a trail littered with the bodies of dead horses, mules, and even unfortunate travelers along the fifty-mile trail. Death lurked everywhere in the form of malaria, yellow fever, and cholera. Of the thousands of forty-niners who attempted the Panama crossing, many died of disease and never made it out of the jungle. Those that survived eventually made it to Panama City, a small outpost on the Pacific coast. Regular passenger service to San Francisco began in late 1849. Before that, thousands of gold seekers became stranded in Panama City for days or even weeks. When ships arrived, miners swarmed them. Often, forty-niners paid extremely high prices for passage. But most thought it was worth it. They were headed to California, the land of gold. And they were sure they'd strike it rich as soon as they arrived. Many ships made only a handful of trips between Panama and San Francisco, as finding captains and crews became increasingly difficult. Ships would arrive, drop anchor in San Francisco and left to rot in place, abandoned by gold seekers seeking riches.

Years later, French attempts to build a canal through Panama advanced further. Led by Ferdinand de Lesseps, the builder of the Suez Canal in Egypt, the French began excavating in 1880. Malaria, yellow fever, and other tropical diseases conspired against the de Lesseps campaign and after nine years and a loss of over 20,000 lives and millions in today's dollars, the French attempt to build a canal went bankrupt.

Despite such setbacks, American interest in a canal grew. Panama was a part of Colombia until 1902. During the previous eighty years, a secessionist movement on the isthmus had swelled. There was a definite movement among residents that Panama needed to break away from Columbian rule.

By 1902, Colombia had been in the grip of a civil war spanning over two years, and Panama had enough. The United States had already decided that it was going to build a canal through Panama, even after a French attempt to do so had failed in the 1880s. It was this French attempt, that prompted Theodore Roosevelt to negotiate with Colombia for the rights to continue France's work. These negotiations came to nothing as Colombia rejected American advances for a deal. This prompted the US to look at helping Panama achieve its independence from Colombia.

Following heated debate over the location of the proposed canal, in 1902, the U.S. Senate voted in favor of building the canal through Panama. Within six months, Secretary of State John Hay signed a treaty with Colombian Foreign Minister Tomás Herrán to build the new canal. The financial terms were unacceptable to Colombia's congress, and it rejected the offer.

President Theodore Roosevelt responded by dispatching U.S. warships to Panama City and Colón in support of Panamanian independence. Panama declared independence in 1903. The newly declared Republic of Panama provided the United States with a ten-mile wide strip of land for the canal and received a one-time, ten-million-dollar payment to Panama and an annual annuity of $250,000. The United States also agreed to guarantee the independence of Panama.

The construction project, from start to completion, took around 10 years, an incredible feat. In addition to initial issues surrounding the recruitment of laborers, due to the canal's questionable early safety record, one of the major difficulties in completing the project was tackling the continental divide, a natural barrier of hard rock, rising to more than three hundred feet high. Massive mechanical steam shovels eventually cut through the continental divide, dubbed the 'Culebra Cut'.

As construction of the canal wore on, employment in the Panama Canal Zone had swelled into huge numbers, bringing with them townships and businesses. Upon completion, thousands of workers were laid off and townships demolished, forcing businesses to close since the project had never set out to be a sustainable employer.

When the canal opened, it was unanimously hailed as an incredible achievement and a marvel of the modern world. Shipping patterns quickly changed and merchandise flowed freely between the U.S. and other naval countries.

The canal cut approximately 7,800 miles off the sea journey from San Francisco to New York, making shipping cheaper, faster, and safer.

Completed in 1914, the Panama Canal symbolized U.S. technological prowess and economic power. Although U.S. control of the canal eventually became an irritant to U.S.-Panamanian relations, at the time it was heralded as a major international foreign policy achievement.

Southernmost Son

Wayne Gales

6

Dad gave me a fair warning about what to expect when we got to the Panama Canal. With this one bottleneck gathering ships from all over the Pacific and Atlantic as the only easy way to get from one ocean to the other, this place was bustling with traffic twenty-four hours a day. "When we transited last time, our little sailboat had to buddy up with some larger boats to get through the locks," he remembered. "Now, with the *Seaglass* at a hundred and fifty-five feet, we're one of the 'big guys'. We get to transit through both the Atlantic and Pacific locks by ourselves, but we have to pay big boat fees."

I couldn't help but notice how nervous my dad was as he looked up when we passed under the Bridge of the Americas. "What are you looking at?" I asked.

"The last time we came this way, some very bad customers were watching us when we passed under that bridge," he pointed up. "When we came back through they jacked us and tried to arrange an early departure from this earth for Karen and me. If it hadn't been for a convenient hurricane, we wouldn't be here."

"I remember the story," I answered. "You even sort of switched identities with their dead bodies." I thought back for a minute. "Even *I* thought you were dead that time." Then I thought it might be a good idea to get that bad memory out of his mind and distract him a little.

"Hey, wasn't there something about pirates in Panama once?" I knew a history lesson was coming but it was good to get his mind on something else. He lapsed right back into teacher-speak.

"As long as this land has been populated, it's been a magnet for pirates, especially on the Caribbean side," Dad started. Looking up at the sky as if history was written in the clouds, I could tell where I got that habit from. "After all, the transit from the Pacific to the Atlantic was a heck of a lot shorter than the overland route from Acapulco to Veracruz, but disease, mosquitos, and everything else in the jungle that stung, bit, or wanted to eat you made this route dangerous for a lot more reasons than pirates." He went on, "I suspect the pirate story you heard about was one of the Golden Age of Piracy's most swashbuckling tales: the sack of Panama City by the pirate Henry Morgan in 1671."

"Now, that's the name I remember, Henry Morgan," I recalled.

Dad smiled and nodded. "It didn't seem possible for even the toughest pirate captain to lead a band of cutthroats through seventy miles of jungle and launch a successful attack on one of Spain's wealthiest ports. But the privateer Henry Morgan made a good attempt of it, assembling an armada of thirty-eight ships off the island of Hispaniola and recruiting more than two thousand buccaneers to the cause, English, French, Dutch, virtually every pirate and privateer in the Caribbean. Their destination was the rich mainland coast of Spain's empire in the Americas."

"Privateer?" I asked. "What's the difference between a privateer and a pirate?"

"It's like the thin line between wreckers and pirates," Dad answered. "Your ancestors blurred that line anytime there weren't enough wrecks to salvage. They conveniently 'made' a wreck by luring a ship close to shore or onto a reef, sometimes with lights hung between mules to make it look as if another ship was safely closer to shore. A privateer was commissioned by governments to attack and plunder enemy countries. England hired people to attack Spain and Spanish privateers attacked England, Portugal and the Dutch, and so on. A pirate robbed from the rich and gave to themselves. Any flag was game." Smiling, he pointed out, "The difference between a pirate and a privateer depends on which side you were on." I was glad my questions got his mind off dark memories.

"So back to Henry," he continued. "Plundering and looting along the way, the pirates sacked the fortress at San Lorenzo, on Panama's Caribbean coast. From there they turned inland, up the Chagres River, and along this very way we're heading," he pointed to the southwest to where Panama City lay waiting. "Every year, fabulous Incan treasures would arrive at this port along with tons of gold and precious stones from Peru and silver from the mines at Potosí. They were stockpiled before being shipped on to Spain. Here was a prize well worth the taking, or at least it would have been if the governor had not been tipped off that the pirates were on their way."

"As it was, most of the good stuff was packed onto galleons, and hidden away in the Islas de las Perlas, an archipelago of two hundred twenty tropical islands, thirty miles out in Panama Bay. Along with the riches, Panama City's wealthiest citizens took refuge there too. The pirates struck at dawn, emerging from the jungle and overwhelming the town's remaining few outnumbered defenders. A month-long orgy of fire, torture, and pillage followed before the pirate hordes left, carrying their meager booty back down the trail to where their fleet waited on the Caribbean shore."

"So, I saw a TV show where they were searching in the jungle for Morgan's booty," I pointed out. "Will it ever be found?"

"How often do you see guys like me, or Mel Fisher's people, or dozens of other legitimate treasure hunters look for buried pirate treasure, or for that matter, ever find any?" Dad asked.

"You've got a point there," I admitted. "They look for shipwrecks, but I have rarely heard professionals chase for pirate riches. Why is that?"

"Because pirates hardly ever buried treasure, they spent it on food, drink, women, and overall good times. They weren't exactly known for the habit of saving for a rainy day, you know."

We continued, on through the locks, across Gatun Lake, and through the Pacific locks until the sights of Panama City came in to view. When we pulled into the St Andrews Bay Yacht Harbor in Panama City, I was more than surprised. My vision of Panama City was a sleepy village with old men in leather huarache sandals walking around in white Guayaberas and linen pants topped with fashionable Panama hats. (I found out later that Panama hats weren't created in Panama. They were originally from Ecuador but were so popular with construction workers during the building of the Panama Canal, that they became associated with Panama, and the name caught on.) Panama City was huge, with high rises everywhere. From the harbor, it looked as big and impressive as Miami, and according to my dad, was home to over a million and a half people.

Pointing south across Bahia de Panama, he answered my puzzled look before I asked. "Old Panama City, what's left of it is over that way. There's nothing left but the ruins of Panama Viejo, just an old tower and some remains of adobe walls."

I peered into the distance and imagined Morgan and his pirates ransacking the old village while the rich people hid on an island a few miles out in the Pacific with their values, turning one of the most famous pirate raids in history more or less a bust.

Safely berthed in the yacht harbor, we topped off our fuel, since we couldn't use sails to transit the canal, added water, and found a local chandler to help us stock up on provisions for the remainder of the trip to Acapulco. We took a two-day break in Panama City and caught up on sleep after enduring twelve on and twelve off since we left Key West. We set sail on the morning of the third day. Leaving the west coast of the isthmus, we had to sail south, then west, before turning north around the Azuero Peninsula.

Looking first at the ship's navigation system, dad looked at me. "Okay Einstein, calculate the trip from here to Acapulco. I've got it at 1278 nautical miles."

"Lessee," I screwed my eyes up toward the clouds again. "The forecast shows some favorable trades, so we can make twelve knots under sail, I think. That means we can rendezvous with David and the *Never on Saturday* in, ah a hundred and six point five hours." I looked at Bric with satisfaction. "Let's say a little less than five days, give or take a thunderstorm."

Dad grinned. "I might as well throw this nav system in the ocean," he laughed. "You can calculate the answer in your head quicker than I can punch in the numbers."

We actually did a little better than twelve knots and got within radio range of the *Saturday* in four days. Anchoring a short distance away from the yacht, we took our Zodiac over and climbed up the same chain ladder used by Levi John when we were off the coast of Port Au Prince, Haiti.

We boarded Moishe's 144 foot, *Never on Saturday*. At first glance, she looked the farthest thing imaginable from a salvage boat, but she had a few tricks up her sleeve. At the stern was a big enclosure that held two mailboxes, curved tubes that are lowered electronically so the propellers divert prop wash. They can point a few thousand horsepower straight down and blow overburden all the way down to bedrock. On her upper deck was another enclosure to hold the most exotic drone I've ever seen, affectionally called FRED, short for Fucking Ridiculous Electronic Device. She was a very capable, and comfortable, salvage vessel.

After a warm greeting, I looked around for the rest of the crew. "Where's Moishe and Golda?" I asked.

David looked a little guilty. "After a little discussion, I convinced the old man that he was past his treasure-hunting days," David admitted. "And Golda almost can't walk anymore. Neither of them needs to be on a rolling deck in rough seas. I got them safely housed in an assisted living community in Miami." He added with a little grin. "It took me, a phone call from Mallory, and a near intervention by Mr. Goodman to convince them, and as it was, I nearly had to tie Moishe to his wheelchair to get him off the *Saturday,*" he added. "They will be a lot safer there, if not as happy."

"Mal never told me," I said with concern.

"I think she thought you guys might not come if they weren't along," David answered, a little embarrassed.

"So you know the exact location of this wreck you wrote to us about?" I asked, changing the subject and excited about getting my hands on more treasure. The last wreck had an amazing yield in gold Escudos, even if they were collected for someone else.

David looked embarrassed again. "Well, not exactly. Just like the old man not being with us on the trip, when I got here and couldn't find the people that found it, I was also afraid you guys wouldn't come if I told you."

Dad looked hurt. "Since when do you think we would ignore an invitation to hunt for treasure just because you don't have hard proof? Did it stop us in Haiti? David, you should be ashamed."

David looked relieved and brightened the moment by rolling out a chart on a table. We gathered around the chart. He turned to my dad, and explained, "I'm sure you know about the Manila Galleons. They carried silks, porcelain, spices, and other trade goods from the Orient via a route from the Pacific and landed in Acapulco or Panama City where they unloaded and collected silver and gold for the return route to pay for more goods." He went on, "Over forty ships were lost in the two hundred and fifty-years the trade route was run. Only a dozen or so have ever been found, and most of them documented and found on the route from the Orient. I suspect as many were lost on the return trip from the Americas, all carrying gold, silver, and emeralds instead of perishable cargo as were lost on the inbound voyages, but only a few have been located."

"Why?" I asked. It didn't make sense to me.

"There are multiple reasons," David answered. "The route crosses into deeper waters not far from shore, and record-keeping in the Americas was not as well documented, or the records were lost in fires. Ships would leave this coast, and never be heard from again, or for that matter, missed." With a little laugh, he added, "It's not like they had the internet or six o'clock news back in those days. The Spanish government in Manila knew within a few months when a ship was expected to return, but wouldn't be surprised if it was two or three years. If they never came back, they would never know if it came to grief on the way to the Americas, on the way back, or where it might be."

It was time to get David off the history lesson. "So what makes you think there's an undocumented wreck?" I asked. "Like my dad says, it's a big ocean. Like looking for a needle in a haystack in an ocean full of haystacks."

"You remember that Grandpa told you he had some success in the Pacific? I'm not at liberty to reveal exactly what he found, but let's just say it helped him move from that floating junkyard he was living on to the *Never on Saturday*." David looked nervous. "Enough said about that. I've probably told you more than I should have. Anyway," David said, trying to change the subject. "He was over on this coast for a few years and hired two locals, Luis and Jose to dive for him," Looking at Bric, "As he did with you long ago. Some years after working for Grandpa, they were spearfishing to the south of Acapulco Bay along the coast and ran across what appeared to be a galleon wreck with ballast stones, cannon, and an anchor. Being on the UNESCO World Heritage list, they knew the wreck was off-limits. It wasn't until a few years later they realized there were no documented eighteenth-century galleon wrecks in that area. They remembered the anchor shape, and realized it might be a Manila Galleon."

"What's UNESCO?" I asked, not recognizing the word.

Dad answered for David. This information was something dear to him. He lapsed into what I call teacher-speak again and made me feel like I was back in the 9th grade. "A UNESCO World Heritage Site is a landmark or area with legal protection by an international convention administered by the United Nations Educational, Scientific and Cultural Organization. World Heritage Sites are designated by UNESCO for having cultural, historical, scientific, or any other form of significance," he added. "There are nearly two hundred countries that have become members, including the US in some areas. They knew that wreck would be untouchable if they reported it, but also knew Moishe had accomplished a work-around before, and mentally noted the location for possible salvage in the future. They've been trying for years to reach my grandfather, but as you know, he's never been electronically sophisticated. He doesn't have a cellphone or even an email. He even changed boats since he's been here. They finally posted a message on Facebook and some treasure hunters in South Florida saw it and got in touch with Moishe."

"Why aren't the wrecks we've worked in the Florida Keys off limits?" I asked.

David was quick to answer. "The United States, thank heaven, has chosen not to give up their sovereignty to the UN, so what we find in territorial waters is OURS, less whatever cut the state gets. Remember Uncle Sugar tried to take the *Atocha* loot from Mel Fisher and the case went all the way to the Supreme Court." I saw dad smile smugly. "You know how THAT turned out."

"So if these are all UNESCO-protected wrecks, how do we work this one?" I asked. "I don't relish sitting in a Mexican prison for the next thirty years becoming some gang's bitch. I've got plans."

"You just have to pay the right people to look the other way and turn the operation into a 'cultural preservation exercise'," David explained. "Years ago, when he was on this coast, Grandpa learned which wheels to grease."

I slowly started coming to a realization. "Wait a minute," I said to David. "We've been down this road before with crooked officials, and it almost cost your sister's life, got my ass shot, and saw my dad look down the business end of a forty-four more than once." I shook my head. "This could be a deal-breaker."

David held up both hands in a 'stop' motion. "What happened in Haiti was an opportunistic thug looking for a one-time quick buck. This is a whole different scene. These people are government officials well-versed in the philosophy of payoffs. It even has a name, '*Mordida*'. It's the way things get done down here. Come to think of it," he added, "It's almost the *only* way to get things done. We've already made a deal and paid the right people upfront in Yankee dollars. If there is such a thing, these politicians are honest crooks. I promise you they will break their neck looking the other way." David smiled, "It looks like my grandfather steered me toward the right politicians." David folded his arms with a smug look. "We're clear to hunt."

"Do you know what might be down there?" I asked.

"It's a guess but a good one," David answered. "Any ship south of Acapulco must have already made the trip from the Far East, made port, unloaded her trade goods, and re-loaded with bullion for the return voyage so she could trade for more merchandise, as they did for over two and a half centuries. Either she was loaded and leaving, or she was going from Acapulco to the second port in Panama. Regardless, she would have been full of silver and gold, either in the form of ingots or coins. There's just no other reason a galleon would be located to the south of here."

I considered this and had another question, "What makes you think it was a wreck from the eighteenth century?"

David looked at his notes and answered, "The two divers told Moishe that they've made a good living escorting rich gringos to dozens of the well-documented sites. Based on the many wrecks they have visited over the years, the shape of the cannons, anchors, and all the ballast stones made it clear it was a galleon, and old. They also saw some broken porcelain cups."

That made David frown. "Any porcelain should have been off-loaded in Acapulco, but," he added, "It might have been dishes and cups for the captain and officers, or could have been cargo destined for Panama, to be carried by mule to South America. Either way, it's worth diving on."

I was growing tired of all the speculation. Standing up, I said, with a stretch, "Dad and I have been twelve on twelve off for a few weeks. I could use a little nap. After that, what you have is good enough for me, let's get moving first thing in the morning," I remembered my gear. "It will take a few trips to get my stuff over from the yacht tomorrow. After a good night's sleep, we'll go find that wreck and start blowing in the afternoon if we're lucky."

I wish I had my dad's ability to sleep anyplace and anywhere. It's normally not that easy for me, but this time I was out like a light almost before I hit the pillow. Ah, wonderful sleep.

Except for that dream.

It seemed like every time I lapsed into this recurring story, the details got more specific and vivid. Oh, the basics were the same, a long hallway, metal floors, someone with me that I couldn't identify, and several doors on each side of the hall. This time I was counting. One, two, three on the left, one, two three, four on the right. I had tried each door, one at a time, and they opened to empty rooms. Somehow I knew that door five would open, too. I put my hand on the lever and pulled it down. We walked into the room quietly. This time, someone was standing over the person in the chair with a gun in hand. The standing man heard us, turned, and raised his gun, aiming it our way.

Boom, Boom, Boom! I sat up in my bed, covered in sweat, then heard the noise again. Boom, Boom, Boom. "Brody!" Called a voice, hammering the cabin door. "Are you gonna sleep all morning?" I groaned, recognizing my dad's voice. "I'll be out in a minute. I need a shower first."

Showered, shaved, and ready for a day in the water, I found out when I emerged from the cabin, that I had missed one of my three favorite meals of the day. Breakfast. Thankfully, *The Saturday*'s chef, affectionately named Hop Sing by Moishe Cohen, came to the rescue. He had banked off some sausage, bacon, biscuits, and knocked together three eggs for a proper breakfast. After my snack, I wandered out on the deck where Bric and David were huddled over that chart again.

"Good afternoon," Dad said sarcastically. "We were beginning to worry. Was it too good of a dream to wake up from?"

"Ah, something like that," I answered, trying to hide my concern. I was beginning to believe it was less than a dream, but more of a premonition. It was too believable and too recurring. Changing the subject was my best reply. Looking up toward the drone hangar, I asked, "Is FRED the drone ready to fly?"

David grinned, finally with some good news. "FRED's ready and upgraded from his last duty. We've graduated to new and better technology."

"Like what?" Dad asked suspiciously. "FRED seemed like a pretty useable tool before. It sure found us the *Conception* in Haiti once we knew where to look."

"We had documents that told us the *Conception* had already been salvaged centuries ago," David reminded me. "We knew most of the ferrous metal, like most of the cannon, anchors, and any other metals would have already been pulled up, even though we eventually did find some, so we were looking more for structure than metal. I'm pretty sure the wreck we're looking for has never been worked or even found for that matter, so we should be able to find lots of ferrous metal, cannons, anchors, and the like."

Almost boasting David added, "As far as equipment, we've modernized with the latest technology, and with less downtime for changing batteries and USB thumb drives." He added, "As they say, the only difference between men and boys, is the price of their toys, and with this toy, they ain't kidding."

Motioning us up the stairs, he led us to the little hanger where FRED lived. Opening the doors we saw the familiar drone perched inside.

Like a hawker standing in front of a nudie bar, he announced, "Gentlemen, meet the newest in undersea exploration." He pointed under FRED at a sleek rocket-looking gadget hanging there.

"The MagArrow is our first-ever UAS-enabled magnetometer and it's setting a new standard for magnetic surveys. The MagArrow is engineered to simplify surveys that are difficult due to the various limitations of pilot-on-board reviews in full-sized aircraft. It consists of an aerodynamic, light-weight carbon fiber shell with internal electronics including magnetic sensors. It's capable of highly precise measurements in an extremely lightweight and tiny package that easily fits under FRED."

Holding his arms wide in a grand gesture, he continued.

"Operation is simple. The drone flies a pattern, as we did in Haiti, while the MagArrow scans the bottom for anything magnetic. Once work is completed and FRED lands back on *Saturday*, the MagArrow handshakes wirelessly with the computer, and data from the MagArrow downloads to the computer instead of pulling a USB thumb drive. So much quicker and cleaner. All we need to do after each pass is swap batteries on FRED, send him off for another pattern, and read the previous pass's data while it's gone. We can cover a heck of a lot more bottom in a lot less time."

"I'll take your word for it," I said after David finished talking, already bored with the mumbo-jumbo. "All this technology is Chinese to me." Nodding toward Hop Sing, I added, "No offense, Chef." With a bow, he replied, "And none taken, Broderick"

Ignoring me, David went on, "It can find something as small as an iron spike at depths up to three hundred feet, although this wreck is no deeper than about fifty-five, according to Luis and Jose."

"Any bad news?" I asked.

David's brow furrowed a little like he was thinking hard. "Ah, there's a couple of *tiny* issues," he admitted. "At the time, our diver friends didn't exactly note the *exact* location of the wreck," he said, almost sheepishly. Then he repeated what he told us last night, "And it's been quite a few years since they were at the wreck. When they first found it, they assumed it was a site that had been long ago discovered, and under the UNESCO umbrella so they just cruised on by and forgot about it. It wasn't until much later that they learned that no wreck, old or recent, had been documented in that general area. It came to them that it was both possibly something valuable and that it might be of interest to Moishe. By then there had been so many other dives, they couldn't remember the exact spot. They said 'sort of' where they saw the debris, within a few miles or two." Holding his arms wide again, he mimicked my dad, and added, "I don't need to tell you 'sort of' can cover a helluva lot of ocean. We'll have to search, but," pointing at the little hanger, "We have the best technology. There's only a limited number of shallow spots in that area that a ship might have grounded on to the south of Acapulco. We should find only a few areas to search thoroughly, but," he cautioned. "There's always the possibility that it didn't sink because it hit something at all."

"Any idea what ship we're looking for?" Dad asked.

"I can make an educated guess," David answered. "The two divers said they saw several large cannons, a big ballast pile, and more than one big anchor, so it should be one of the big Manila Galleons." David rolled out a spreadsheet he had made. While we looked over his shoulder, he explained, "Over forty ships were lost across the two hundred and fifty years that the trade route was used. Here's a list of the ships that have been found. There were several more that went missing but were never found. I'm guessing she could be the *San Marcos de Leon*, one of the biggest of the Manila Fleet to ever sail. She left Manila in 1745 and was never seen again. Some of the records in Acapulco were lost to a fire, but based on the location to the south of the bay," he explained, pointing south. "She got to Acapulco, unloaded her cargo, took on a load of gold and silver, then wrecked not far out of port, either bound for Panama to pick up more goods or hit some uncharted rock while on her way back to the Philippines." As he folded up the spreadsheet, he added. "If she is the *San Marcos*, she would be full of silver bars, coins, and gold, all ripe for the taking. Like I said before, we just needed to, as they say, 'compensate' the right people." David added with a smile.

Here we go again.

Southernmost Son

Wayne Gales

7
Flashback, June 1745

The *Nao de Acapulco Galleon, San Marcos de Leon* cast off her lines from the wharf in Manila, taking advantage of an outgoing tide to help her clear the harbor. One of the largest such galleons ever built, she was over a hundred and fifty feet long and displaced over two thousand tons. Built forty years earlier in Mexico, she was well-armed to discourage pirates and hosted a crew of over four hundred sailors. Contrary to popular belief, Spanish galleons were not crewed solely by Spanish seamen, but by a mixture of Chinese, Philippine, South Seas Islanders, and black slaves. With a myriad of languages spoken, each nationality was managed by a multi-lingual crew boss, and the different ethnicities kept aloof from other nationalities and cooked their own food, what little there was. In her holds, the *San Marcos* carried all sorts of cargo. Though Chinese silk was by far the most valuable cargo, other exotic goods, such as perfumes, porcelain, cotton fabric from as far as India, precious stones, silks, hand-painted tableware, prized spices, and other goods, all bound to be unloaded in Acapulco or occasionally Panama. Then carried by hand or mule back to the east coast of Mexico for transit to Mother Spain by a different fleet of ships, or from Panama, by land, south into the settlements there. The goods had been traded in the Far East for silver, gold, emeralds, pearls, and other cargo, and brought to the New World on the *Nao de China* leg of the voyage. With luck, a galleon could make a round-trip voyage in a year, but weather and other factors dictated it could take twice that long.

As misfortune would have it, currents, prevailing winds, and the reluctance that crews had of straying too far from land when dictated a circuitous route, sailing north from the Philippines near the Japanese coast before striking east across the Pacific. The bad fortune was compounded when malaria-infected mosquitos flew aboard the ship when they passed a semi-tropical island in the Pacific, starting the spread of infection aboard the ship that grew constantly worse.

The two youngest members of the crew had become friends, sharing their meager daily rations and water, huddled below decks in the night as sickness and death surrounded them. Francisco was on his second voyage and had signed on as an apprentice at the bidding of his wealthy Spanish parents at the age of fifteen, leaving his home town of Acapulco assigned to the *piloto* or pilot, a grizzled, stern, forty-year-old master with decades of experience. Francisco knew that with luck, he would be allowed to briefly take the huge wheel of the galleon, giving his master a brief break in ten or fifteen years, but for now, he was relegated to bringing water and running errands to the crew on behalf of the helmsman during the day, and only occasionally was allowed to touch the ship's wheel, feeling the great vessel react to the pilot's skills. At night, when not on duty, he had no true berth but found refuge among the sacks of dry goods in the hold to sleep.

His friend was only eleven and on his second voyage as a cabin boy. The youngest member of the crew and the lowest in the hierarchy. He was abandoned as a young child by his destitute parents in the streets of the village of Krung Thep Maha Nakhon, present-day Bangkok, Thailand. He was plucked from the streets a few years later by Dutch traders and brought on board their ship as a cabin boy, cleaning slops, bringing food to the crew, and any other task considered beneath able-bodied seamen. His inability to communicate with the European sailors resulted in frequent cuffs and whippings.

He sneaked ashore when the ship called on Manila and reverted to his streetwise habits. Barely ten years old, lice-infested, and covered in scabs. He was slowly starving and would have been dead in a few weeks in Manila. He was wandering the streets, holding a wooden bowl and walking from sailor to sailor uttering the only word he knew in Spanish, begging "*dinero? dinero?*" (The Spanish word for money). Desperate for crew members, the boy was picked up one night, bound, and brought on board the *Leon,* as an unwilling cabin boy. After sailing with the tide, the crew laughed at the little boy and untied him, not knowing they were dealing with a small, but experienced sailor. "He doesn't know Spanish," remarked the first mate. "What do we call him?" Not understanding the conversation, he held his hands out, cupped them, and uttered, "*dinero?*" Laughingly, the crew announced that must be his name, so Dinero, he became from then on.

Life aboard the *Leon* was hardly better than the streets of Krug Thep or Manila, but at least he got a few scraps of leftover food, an occasional hard dry biscuit, and a sip of dirty water every day.

Normally, the Manila Galleons would take three or four months from the time they left sight of the Japanese coast until the west coast of North America came into view, but the ship was not so fortunate on this voyage. Storms and inconsistent tradewinds left the ship adrift in the north Pacific for weeks, and it took nearly nine months to transit the longest leg of the journey. The *Leon* finally neared the coast of present-day California. They came in sight of the coast not far south of the magnificent harbor where decades later the village of Yerba Buena, known in modern times as San Francisco was settled. The trade route never saw what became known as the Golden Gate. In fact, the only map of California aboard the *San Marcos*, drawn by Nicolas de Fer in 1720 must have mistaken the entrance to San Franciso Bay as a peninsula that connected to the Gulf of California in Baja. The map showed the landmass as an island!

They anchored in the tranquil bay surrounded by cypress trees that later became known as Monterey, at that time, still unsettled by Europeans. By then, nearly half the passengers and crew were dead from scurvy, starvation, and malaria, a devastating disease that eventually created severe anemia, kidney failure, and eventually death.

The galleons never established trade relations with the dozens of coastal native tribes that populated the area, instead choosing to shoot game, waterfowl, and the occasional Indian. Had they befriended the multitude of tribes, they would have traded, among other things, for bread made from acorn flour, high in vitamin C, unknown at that time as a cure and preventative for scurvy. Even with freshly caught game on board, the sailors continued to starve on the protein-rich lean meat, and it became questionable if the *Leon* would have enough able-bodied sailors to successfully make it to their destination. Asian crew members fared a little better, supplementing their diet with fresh-caught fish, a healthier diet, but it didn't keep them from the ravages of malaria.

They continued south along the uninhabited coast, passing through the Channel Islands Strait, near Santa Rosa Island. A week later, the ship sailed by present-day San Diego harbor, then along the arid land known now as Baja California. Eventually sighting the *El Arco*, the familiar stone arch landmark gracing today's tourist Mecca, Cabo San Lucas. As they rounded the tip of the peninsula the *Leon* was only another week's voyage to their final destination in Acapulco. Southernly trade winds favored the galleon as she approached Acapulco Harbor, but a strong outgoing tide meant it would take expert sailing by the crew to avoid overshooting the mouth of the bay, and there was barely enough healthy crew to maneuver the lumbering ship.

Southernmost Son

Wayne Gales

8

I was raring to start searching for the wreck that very afternoon, but this is Mexico. Even though we weren't locals, the 'manana' mentality started to take control of David and my dad almost immediately.

"First, we need to find the two divers, Luis and Jose, who told Moishe about that galleon," David said. Turning to me he added, "I don't care how good you are. Mallory isn't here to buddy dive with you. She called before you got here and gave me strict instructions not to let you dive alone or your dad go underwater anymore." Pop looked pissed but kept his mouth shut when he remembered how he would endure 'the wrath of Mallory' if he disregarded her instructions.

David ignored Dad's looks and continued, "I'm sure Luis and Jose are still in Acapulco, but I have no idea how to reach them. I'll bet if we visit a few local dive shops and grease the wheels with some pesos, they will tell us where to find them, or at least tell them how to find us." Handing Bric and me a handful of hundred-peso notes and a list, he instructed. "You two should split up so you can cover all the shops in one day. According to the internet, Acapulco has at least a dozen dive shops, probably more."

"That's a lot of cash just to find a couple of locals," I remarked, counting the colorful money with an image of a Native American on the front. "It's monopoly money" answered David. "A hundred pesos is worth about fifty cents. Offer one or two thousand to someone who will lead you to our boys. I'll guess just about everyone in town knows them or knows who they are."

Early the next morning, David brought the *Saturday* to a berth in the harbor, and after taking the Zodiac back to *Seaglass*, we followed to a spot next to him. We had to go through the rigmarole my father told me about when they docked in Belize years ago, paying for dockage and a full-time watchman, then a little more for someone else to watch the watchman. After securing the ships, Dad and I hailed a taxi at the entrance to the yacht harbor, *Club de Yates*. It was only a ten-minute ride to the middle of the city. The main drag along the beach, *Avenida Costera Miguel Aleman*, was littered with high-rise hotels and we could have been in Miami, (except more people here spoke English). Following David's plan, we split the town in two. The locals were friendly and eager to point me toward the dive shop addresses, but when I got to the first place, I encountered a major problem. When I walked into the shop and announced in English that I was looking for two local divers, everyone turned away in suspicion and suddenly lost their ability to understand me. It was obvious I was using the wrong tactic, so at the next address, I tried a different approach.

"A friend of mine was down here a few years ago and hired two divers. I would like to hire them too. Does anyone know Luis and Jose?" This almost worked too well. It seemed *nobody* claimed to know the duo, and *everyone* claimed to be better divers than the guys they didn't know.

Like I said, this was going nowhere fast.

Dad and I had agreed to meet for lunch before we split up. Even though neither of us had ever set foot in Acapulco, Dad came up with the name of a restaurant in a hotel, seemingly out of the blue. At noon, I made my way back toward the beach. I couldn't help but think how much fun this adventure would have been if Mallory had been along. Despite her request that I kiss strange girls no more than once, I had no intention to kiss any pretty *señoritas*. I don't have eyes for anyone after falling in love with the most beautiful, sweetest, kindest, smartest person, I've ever met, but when I got to the restaurant, it was obvious Bric had no such moral boundaries. Walking up to me with a young *señorita* under each arm, he said with a disarming smile. "Ah son, would it be okay if you had lunch on your own?" Handing me his list of dive shops, he added, "You don't mind hitting the last four stores for me this afternoon, do you? Seems like something big has come up."

Neither girl was particularly attractive. In fact, both were downright homely and, as my dad would describe, a tad bit over-nourished and hygienically challenged. When one of them smiled, I could tell she had a mouthful of summer teeth. Summer there, some aren't. Hearing dad slur his words a little, I would guess alcohol may have been involved in his selection process.

"Don't forget," I answered dryly, "I've seen you naked, and in all due respect, Sir, it ain't that big." I thought for a moment and added, "But at your age, if it falls off in two weeks, you won't miss it too much."

"You will learn someday, young man," he answered with a big smile, waggling a finger. "That it's not the size of the wand, but the magic that's in it."

I think he was hoping the girls didn't speak that much gringo. They turned and walked away so fast, I didn't have a chance to ask for his share of the money. As they rounded the corner out of sight, I could hear my dad whistling a tune off-key, a habit I've heard all my life after he's had a few. As they went out of earshot, I recognized the Crosby, Stills, and Nash song, '*If you can't be with the one you love, love the one you're with.*'

I think I know where *his* pesos went. Go for it, Pop.

Jose Cuervo, you are a mortal enemy.

Well, I was still hungry and it takes some work to keep this bulk up. I chose a seat at a small table toward the back. The menu was both in English and Spanish to help the tourists successfully find a meal. *Taco* in English was *Taco* in Spanish and I ordered two. The waiter brought a plate swimming in refried beans, rice, lettuce, and tomato. As I've said before, lettuce isn't *food*, it's what food *eats*. Pushing the hay to one side I devoured the tacos in two minutes, washing it down with a Coke in a glass bottle, something that almost doesn't exist at home.

In the middle of my meal, I felt arms around my neck in a hug. "Looking for a party?" said a voice. I turned in my seat, and someone, *something*, plopped into my lap. She/it reeked of cheap perfume and was wearing makeup that looked like it was put on with a spackle knife. I wasn't sure of the gender. Heck, I wasn't even able to identify the species at that moment. 'She', if it was a she, smelled like the bottom of my grandma's purse. I stood up, untangling myself from the loose jewelry, shooed her away, and sat back down to finish lunch, remembering something I was told long ago. Sex in Mexico is like bungee jumping. They both cost fifty bucks, they both take five minutes and if the rubber breaks, you die.

Just as I finished my meal, I heard someone yell from behind a door, "*Aiee, Lupe, el churro is en la Cocina!*" What smattering of Spanish I knew translated that to 'The goat's in the kitchen!'

I crooked a finger toward the waiter as fast as I could.

A long time ago, probably the first time I had a few dollars in my pocket, my dad, sister, and I went to a popular Mexican restaurant on Stock Island. After a yummy dinner, my dad coached me in Spanish on how to order a special Mexican dessert. "Tell the waiter, *La cuenta por favor.*" I repeated the phrase several times, then repeated it to the server. When she brought me the bill, I knew I'd been hoodwinked, by the best hoodwinker on the island.

"*La cuenta por favor,*" I said to the waiter.

I knew what it meant now.

Southernmost Son

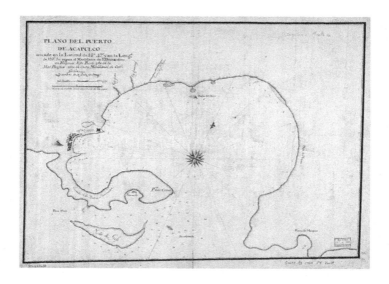

9
Flashback –Acapulco

Acapulco was inhabited by the Nahua Indians (the predecessors of the Aztecs). Recent discoveries have surfaced in the form of Petroglyphs which may indicate even previous settlements around 3000 B.C.

There are even theories about early encounters and commerce with the Chinese culture as early as 412. Although testimonies of this exist in several Chinese records, physical evidence is scarce. The name the Chinese gave Acapulco was "Ye Pa Ti," or the "Place with Beautiful Waters."

The Spanish established a commercial route to Asia in the sixteenth century and selected Acapulco as the eastern terminus of the Manila Galleon route. They built a port and shipbuilding facilities there, taking advantage of its naturally protected, deepwater harbor. For more than two hundred and fifty years, *Naos,* or Spanish trading galleons, made annual voyages from the Philippines to Acapulco and back. Gold, silks, and spices were unloaded in Acapulco and carried overland to Veracruz, which were then loaded onto waiting ships for the transatlantic voyage to Spain. Meanwhile, Dutch and English privateers such as Sir Francis Drake were busy looting the Spanish ships of their valuable cargo. To protect their investment, the Spanish built the Fuerte de San Diego. But it was the Mexican War of Independence, not pirates, that abruptly killed the trade route.

For the next century, Acapulco declined and remained relatively isolated from the rest of the world until a paved road linked it with Mexico City in 1927. Prosperous Mexicans began vacationing here. Hollywood came calling and by the '50s, Acapulco was becoming a glitzy, jet-set resort. But by the 1970s, overdevelopment and overpopulation had taken their toll, and the bay became polluted with raw sewage. Foreign tourists took their cash to the newer resorts of Cancún and Ixtapa. Once again, Acapulco's heyday was over.

Wayne Gales

In the late 1990s, the city launched ambitious revitalization programs, pouring millions into cleaning up the bay. The big break came in 2002, when American college students, attracted by cheap rooms and a welcoming hotel industry, began coming to Acapulco in droves, replacing Cancún as Mexico's top Spring Break hot spot. Today, Acapulco's beaches are fronted with high-rise luxury hotels, and evidence of its glory as the eastern terminus of two hundred and fifty years of lucrative trade from China has all but disappeared.

Southernmost Son

Wayne Gales

10

After leaving the restaurant with the goat-filled kitchen, *(Heaven knows if one of the goat's cousins made it into my tacos)*, I took a cab to the next dive shop. With the rest of my list and almost all of my dad's, there would be no more walking if I was going to get this job done before closing time. The results at the next store were the same as before. Either Luis and Jose had flown the coop or I was asking the wrong questions. I was running out of bribe money fast and I was striking out faster than an old major league pitcher with a bad arm.

Just before five, I had only one shop left on Dad's list. Without much hope of success, I entered the door. Cutting right to the chase, when I walked in, I stopped and announced to the room in loud English, "I have a thousand pesos for anyone that can help me find two divers named Luis and Jose." I added, "A friend recommended them."

A wiry, bandy-legged smallish man with salt and pepper hair, much older than most of the people in the shop, walked up to me. He looked more Asian than Mexican. One of the few things I absorbed in high school was that Native Americans were descended from Asians, crossing a land bridge between Siberia and Alaska long ago.

"What's your friend's name?" He asked in very good English. I figured a straight answer was worth a try. "Moishe Cohen," I answered. Without expressing recognition, he smiled a little. "I can take you to Jose," he said. "For ten thousand pesos."

I grimaced. Counting the money Bric and David had handed me, I confessed, "I don't have that much left on me." Then, reaching into my wallet, I surveyed the contents. "Would American dollars work?" He nodded eagerly, so I counted out five Ben Franklins, most of my stash. "Keep the change," I offered. "Let's meet Jose. We may have a job for him and his brother."

Pocketing the cash and crooked his finger to follow him. The little Mexican turned and walked out of the dive shop without another word. We walked into a poor neighborhood for another fifteen minutes until he stopped and turned. Holding up a hand he said, "Wait here. I'll get Jose." I stood on the sidewalk as he walked down the alley out of sight. After ten minutes, I began to wonder if I would ever see him or my money again when he emerged, followed by someone who could have been his brother, only a little older.

"Señor, this is Jose. I told him you were sent by Moishe." Shaking my hand vigorously, his first question was one of concern. "The old man, Señor Moishe, he is *muerto* (dead), no?"

"Alive and kicking, last time I saw him," I answered. "From what my dad told me, he's in his late nineties and looks like he's a hundred and twenty. But Moishe and Golda are doing fine, living in Miami. I'm here with their grandson. We hope to find that wreck you and Luis discovered years ago." Curious, I added. "When will I meet Luis?"

"You just did," the other man answered with a big smile, holding out his hand.

I flared anger. "I just paid five hundred bucks to the person I'm gonna hire?"

Louis laughed. "You offered to pay me to find either Luis or Jose. I brought you to Jose. It sounds like a fair deal to me."

I had to smile inwardly to myself. He had me there. I needed to learn how to do business in this land of *mañana*.

Understanding I was a little miffed, Luis changed his demeanor. "Señor, let me make it up to you." He took me by the arm and motioned down the street. "Come with us. Let me use some of your money to buy you the best dinner in the world. No tourist food like you would be served on the beach but *real* food."

Thinking of the incident with the goat, I had no intention of returning anywhere near that lunch spot. I didn't hesitate. "Lead the way!" I answered with a laugh.

I followed the brothers inland, away from the beach and farther into the slums that surround the tourist district, into a neighborhood even I wouldn't venture into at night without my escorts. But they seemed comfortable in their surroundings, and the clusters of tough-looking dudes that seemed to hang around every store and taco stand smiled and shook hands with the duo. Obviously respected individuals when we walked by. Luis and Jose looked north of sixty years old, but I almost had to trot to keep up with the wiry brothers. They might look oldish, but they were in shape. After twenty minutes, Luis stopped and held open a door, motioning me inside a shabby green-painted brick building with a hand-painted sign on the front that read *La Fonda Cocina del Madres.* "Fonda has many meanings in Mexico." Jose explained, "To us, it means a local mom-and-pop restaurant and the best food anywhere."

Well, that hole-in-the-wall restaurant didn't look like much, but for about three bucks apiece, from what I could tell, a plate piled with marinated pork, a mountain of rice, and a bowl of refried beans with a foil-wrapped supply of fresh hot tortillas on a paper plate appeared at our table. I would have rather seen a cheeseburger or at least a couple of tacos show up, but my daddy taught me to be polite with strangers, especially those who thought they were doing something nice. He always said '*You ought to dance with those what brung ya.*' I was also very aware that my life might be in their hands under seventy-five feet of water in a few days. Following their lead, I scooped meat, rice, and beans on a tortilla, folded it into a sandwich, and chowed down. After my first bite, I was happily surprised.

This stuff was *tasty!*

Over dinner, we talked a little business. Since David sent me out to find these guys, I considered myself authorized to make a deal. The arrangement was easier to arrive at than I expected. After very little small talk, Luis, who was clearly the spokesman for the duo, cut right to the chase.

"We are honored Señor Moishe remembered us," he started. "We would be happy to work with you and his grandson." Looking at me with a smile, he gave an expressionless deadpan offer. "Two hundred US dollars a day, each, and a portion of any treasure you may find." Leaning back in his chair, he put his arms behind his head in a relaxing gesture. "I trust Señor David is as honorable as his grandfather and will make our portion a reasonable amount."

My curiosity about their facial features was nagging me. I had to ask, "How long have you lived in Acapulco?" I asked. "Forgive me, but you look more like you are Chinese or maybe Japanese than most of the Mexicans I have met down here."

Luis laughed. "Jose and I are, what you gringos would call 'real mutts'. I'm sure you know that all Native Americans came here from Asia as long as 25,000 years ago, but we come from more recent stock. Folklore says we are descended on our father's side from Castilian Spanish *Conquistadores*. Our mother can trace her roots back to the Nahua Indians and a shipwrecked boy from Asia." He pointed in a southerly direction. "The story says he swam ashore when a galleon he was on sank some kilometers south, the only survivor. When we found the wreck you are looking for, we always wondered if that was the ship our ancestor was on." With a distant smile, he added, "It's a fable we may never know was true."

My dad always taught me to be generous with OPM, Other People's Money. I didn't hesitate. Standing up, I shook hands with my new dive buddies, Luis and Jose to formalize the agreement. "She's called the *Never on Saturday*," I advised. "Just look for the second biggest boat in the yacht harbor, you can't miss her. See you at nine a.m. Don't forget your gear." I hesitated for a moment. "You do have your own dive gear?"

Luis answered with a sly smile, "Oh si, Señor Brody, we have everything we need. See you *mañana*!"

Disregarding my instructions our two guides showed up at the yacht three days later. At least they were carrying their gear. The crew quarters would sleep four, but the nights were pleasant and I planned to sleep on deck most of the time unless it was raining. Outfitting the *Saturday* for the salvage operation was not an exercise for either the faint of heart or bank account. Fuel, food, cases, and cases of bottled water, and a supply of liquor were loaded until the ship looked more like a garbage scow than a luxury yacht. Inwardly, I was glad again that this expedition was being footed with Other People's Money.

Pop showed up a day later at the crack of two, chipper and appearing fit as a fiddle, with no apparent after-effects of his mission of transgression. It brought to mind my late Conch uncle, Johnny Russell. I never knew he drank until I saw him sober one night.

We fretted about leaving our precious *Seaglass* alone, maybe for several weeks, but Cookie assured us in broken English, "You go, I be fine." When we walked back up the dock, our last sight of the *Seaglass* was a reassuring one, that of the ancient, diminutive chef sitting on a stool at the top of the gangplank, arms crossed and holding the largest meat cleaver from the galley in his right hand. I didn't doubt he would be sitting in that exact same spot the day we returned.

All loaded, we eased the *Saturday* out of the harbor past Isla de Roqueta. "Where to amigo?" Dad asked Luis, while the three of us stood behind Captain Novak. Pointing south, he answered with some hesitation. "Maybe five or six miles," he answered slowly. "In fifty or sixty feet." (It kept getting a little deeper every time.) "It seems a little strange," Luis mused, "but there's no real reef in that area." He frowned, "Most wrecks we have found or dived on over the years had obviously hit something. This wreck was just lying there in the open, without anything for it to have hit, and at least a mile from shore." Luis looked down apologetically. "I wish we could help more. It's been many years and many dives ago." Smiling, he turned toward my dad, and added, "I'm sure you know, señor Bric when you get a little older, the mind forgets things."

"Do you think pirates might have been the culprit?" I asked, almost hopefully.

"There's no doubt, pirates and privateers were always a threat," my dad answered. "But ships were almost as valuable as the treasure inside. They would take a ship, board it, and either kill or enslave the crew, but sink a priceless galleon like you see in the movies? Never."

I could tell when the brothers were getting uncomfortable with our questions. Changing the subject, I asked, "So both of you worked for Moishe several years ago." Holding my hands wide to indicate the luxurious *Never on Saturday*, I asked, "Your effort must have had some success. According to my dad, he was salvaging in a rust bucket that hardly floated before he upgraded."

This time it was Jose who looked uncomfortable. "Señor Cohen is an honorable man." He said slowly, "Perhaps he'll tell you the story someday."

David broke the awkward silence with a question. "Do either of you have an idea at least *about* where we should start our search?"

Wayne Gales

"Oh si, Señor David," Luis answered, sounding confident this time and eager to break the silence. "Look for a rocky shoreline covered with, how do you say it, *sellos*, fur seals, then offshore to a depth of fifty or sixty feet. He dug in his memory for a moment. Maybe a little south of there, no more than a few miles, I think. Jose and I were free diving, spearfishing for fresh fish to sell to the street markets, and looking for big *langostas*, what you call lobsters. The area near the shore has been picked over, but go a little deeper, and they have never been touched." Grinning with a smile full of gold fillings, he added, "Muy grande. Huge. We could always sell them for good money." Rolling his eyes up to calculate, "Maybe as much as six dollars US to the tourist restaurants."

Yeah, I thought to myself. The same bugs I saw on the menu at the tourist restaurant for 'MP' market price, well over a hundred bucks, when I asked what the market price was.

"Captain Novak," David instructed, "Cruise up the coast close enough to the shoreline so I can spot a seal colony. Watch your depth."

A teensy bit annoyed at David reminding him to watch his depth, a practice he was always diligent at, Novak only gritted his teeth and responded with respect, "Yessir."

We motored south for about an hour while David scouted the shoreline with a big set of Swarovski 12x field glasses. After an hour he passed them off to my eyes, and then both brothers took a turn. We were about to decide we missed our spot when Luis shouted, "There!" He said excitedly, "I see *sellos*! Mucho sellos!" Handing David the binocs, he adjusted the focus and smiled. "I can see the rocks. Lots of seals." Lowering the glasses, he asked Captain Novak, "What's our depth?" The skipper peered at his instruments, "I've been keeping the *Saturday* steady at about forty-five."

"Ease her out due west till she reads fifty," David instructed. "Drop anchor. We'll start running a pattern with FRED in the morning." Picking up the phone he dialed the kitchen. "Won, dinner for eight. We dine as a team tonight."

I was a little surprised when Jose spoke up. "Señor David, could Luis and I contribute to our dinner tonight? As I mentioned, the langostas are plentiful and large this far from shore. We would be happy to supply you with a nice catch." David looked at the two diminutive Mexicans. "Why sure, I think Won would be happy to cook up some lobsters." Turning to me, he added, "Brody, break out the scuba gear for these gentlemen and make sure the tanks are charged. Bric, can you take watch and keep an eye out for unwelcome predators?"

Luis was quick to answer, "Oh no, Señor Brody, we don't need tanks. It's only fifty feet deep. We can free dive easily." Jose added, "We have all we need. Mask, fins, snorkels, a catch bag, tickle sticks, and maybe a pole spear in case a nice grouper shows up." He added, "And a full set of scuba gear when we find the wreck."

This, I wanted to see. I mean, most people struggle to work at fifty feet, much less hunt. I've never met anyone that could match me at such depth, except my dad before he was shot. These guys didn't look like they could hold their breath in a kiddie pool.

Ignoring the ramp that went directly from the crew quarters into the ocean on *Saturday*, the brothers donned their gear and just flipped backward off the side of the yacht with a splash. They took a deep breath and disappeared under the surface. I peeked at my watch when they went under. Dad's eyebrows rose after they were out of sight for a while. Pointing at his dive watch, he commented, "I make it at a little over two minutes now," he added with a little smile, "I guess they don't need tanks."

The brothers both emerged after almost three minutes, each holding two of the largest spiny lobsters I've ever seen. Kicking my Crocs off, I headed for the storage locker. "Man, I'm going to join this fun!" I exclaimed. Dad caught my arm. "Maybe another time," he said gently. "The brothers want to contribute to dinner tonight. Let them enjoy being part of the team."

Looking back, I'm glad I listened.

When the duo headed back down, I noticed they weren't alone anymore. At least a half dozen curious seals had joined them, zooming in graceful circles, stopping curiously in front of the divers, then surfacing to catch a breath and overall enjoying the presence of their strange intruders. "Actually they aren't seals, but sea lions," Dad pointed out, smiling at the antics.

"What's the difference?" I asked. Like my father often does, he turned into a college lecturer. "Sea lions are brown, bark loudly, walk on land using their flippers, and have visible ear flaps. Seals have small flippers, wriggle on their bellies on land, and lack ear flaps."

"Okay," I answered. "That's more than I need to know. A seal is still just a seal to me."

Dad shrugged his shoulders and watched the brothers come up one more time, each with another big lobster. "Dos mas!" Luis shouted, tossing the prickly crustaceans up to us and catching his breath before heading to the bottom one last time. As they slid below in the crystal-clear water, I pointed out to my dad, "You can see them all the way to the bottom."

We continued watching, with David, Captain Novak, Dad, and me leaning over the side like we were on a glass-bottom excursion, when dad said curiously, "Where did the sea lions

go?" I hadn't noticed until he pointed it out. Strange. On the other side of *Saturday*, Won shouted, "There they are!" We all went to the other rail and watched the seal pack, at least a half-dozen of them racing toward the shore, porposing in and out of the swells. "I wonder who rang the dinner bell?" I asked no one in particular. Suddenly one of the sea lions flew at least six feet into the air, its rear half firmly in the grasp of huge jaws. "Great White!" Dad exclaimed as the shark crashed to the surface in a pink bloody foam. The attack was so sudden and violent, that I was speechless. "I've never seen a white," I said slowly. "Uh, maybe we should get the boys out of the water in case that monster wants dessert."

We went back to the other side of the yacht as the brothers surfaced one last time, each with a big lobster. "Peligro! danger!" Dad shouted, getting their attention. "Tiburón! shark!" Tossing the two lobsters up, where they were collected by the cook, you've never seen two people scramble up a ladder faster. "I was Luis in the water." Remarked the brother to me, "But when your father yelled there was a shark, I changed my name to Jesus!" "I wanted to walk on the water!"

David had gone into the lounge during the excitement. "That was Dolly!" he remarked.

"Who?" I asked. "Somebody you dated that got eaten?"

Ignoring my smart-assed remark, he explained. "Dolly's an eleven-foot female Great White shark, caught two years ago by the Monterrey Aquarium near the Farallon Islands off San Francisco, a hotbed for white sharks. And tagged for tracking by OCEARCH."

"Oh-who?" I asked, "and how do you know all of this about a fish you've seen jump once, sending a seal to the promised land?"

"OCEARCH," David replied, patiently, "Is an organization that tags and tracks everything from whale sharks, turtles, white sharks, tiger sharks, and even seals. That's what I was doing in the lounge, checking the laptop. OSEARCH is an organization founded to help scientists collect previously unattainable data in the ocean." Pointing toward the shore he added. "I checked OCEARCH and it confirmed there was a tagged white shark, named Dolly, in the vicinity. I'll go back inside in a little while to report the sighting."

"I'm not afraid of much in the ocean," I pointed out, "But your girlfriend out there ain't on that list. Do we dare play in the water and risk being part of the food chain?"

David smiled. "There are a couple of pluses to this situation. One, thanks to OCEARCH, we know exactly where Dolly is, a bonus we might have never known had she not dined on her favorite food instead of one of us. Unless there's a popular hangout like the Farallons, white sharks like Dolly travel a lot. We just hang around for a few days and with luck, she will be long gone. Two, as long as our sea lion friends are hanging around the *Saturday*, the coast, so to speak, should be clear."

"I like reason 'one' better than reason 'two'," I remarked. "Our furry buddies checked out when they were already a target. I would rather our friend shows she's far, far away before I dip a foot in the water."

Wayne Gales

11

Just to be safe, we avoided getting wet for three days, until Dolly the shark showed on the OCEARCH site that she had moved over two hundred miles north. Anyway, there was no real reason to go diving until FRED found something, other than a desire by Luis and Jose to add fresh food to our menu. The Pacific Ocean in this area was target-rich, to say the least. Along with plentiful lobsters, the boys brought up a constant supply of abalone, freshly speared grouper, calico bass, corbina, and more. You never knew what they might bring up. I thought my dad and I were pretty competent predators, but these boys were *good*.

FRED had to do his job anyway and find this wreck, provided we were in the right neighborhood to start with. I was given the task of designated battery-swapper when the drone came back to the ship every half-hour. When it landed, the data was automatically downloaded to David's desktop for review like he said it would. We were back to hurry up and wait mode. As long as it had taken to find the galleon in Haiti, I didn't have my hopes up for a speedy discovery here in Mexico.

"If Luis and Jose have the right seal rookery, the ship should be nearby," David observed. "They remembered being at about fifty-five feet, and the bottom drops off pretty fast in these waters, which is why the marlin and sail fishing is so good close to Acapulco." He pointed toward the shore. "Mark a line directly out from the seals, plot fifty to sixty feet of depth, and we should be in the right neighborhood. Since the *Leon's* been lying there untouched, it should be loaded with silver, gold, and all kinds of metal. It should be fairly easy to pick up with the MagArrow."

"What kind of shape do you think it's in?" Dad asked.

"Well," David said slowly, scratching his chin. "There's no reef or shallow area around here, and currents are not bad, so whatever made it sink should have left it pretty intact and without a big debris field. Being so close to port in Acapulco Bay, it's not likely that it would have departed the middle of a tropical storm." He shook his head, almost to himself. "There's no earthly reason for a Manila Galleon to sink here. It's a mystery we'll probably never learn." Brightening up he added. "But, you never look a gift horse in the mouth. As long as it's untouched and full of treasure, we recover it, pay off the politicians, and cash in. Cha-ching!"

"I'm good with that," I chimed in. "In the meantime, we hang around and wait."

"That's why they call it 'treasure hunting' instead of 'treasure finding'." Dad pointed out. "It can be weeks, months, or years of looking at a big ocean with nothing to show for your efforts, followed the next moment by an amazing success that makes you forget all the time you spent looking."

The routine continued. I would have far rather been fishing or diving, but my day was cut into thirty-minute segments swapping batteries and jamming the depleted ones in the charger slots.

I would have enjoyed judging a paint-drying contest more.

The breeze and prevailing currents made searching to the south a better option, especially since the waters near and north of Acapulco had been explored extensively over the years. We searched all day, every day, sticking to a logical depth range, according to the brothers, until we were miles south of the seal herd.

"I'm beginning to wonder if this ship was either in your imagination or dreamed up in a cloud of giggle weed," I groused to Luis and Jose after several weeks. "I'm about ready to pack it in and have some more good Mexican food while you guys keep searching." Nodding to my dad's wisdom, I added, holding my arms wide, "Somebody's told me more than once, that it's a big ocean out here."

"Oh, no, Señor Brody," Luis answered in earnest. "We've dived on hundreds of wrecks over the years. We know what we saw." He looked at me seriously, hurt and disappointed that I had even questioned him. "It was a wreck and very old."

David interrupted our argument. "Maybe you two could stop bickering and come take a look at this." Pointing at a big box next to the computer, he put his finger on a green line bouncing up and down on the round screen. "What's that?" I quizzed. "The heartbeat of a horny shark in love?"

"That," he said, ignoring my smart-assed remarks like always, "Is an oscilloscope 'hit' from the MagArrow. We've got metal down there and lots of it. It could indicate a wreck or at least a debris field." Smiling, David referred to the computer and jotted down GPS coordinates. Standing up from the computer, David smiled for the first time in weeks. "Ready to get wet?"

I haven't spent much time diving with foreigners, and I had a vision of the Mexicans in old Voit masks, BC's (buoyancy compensator vests) on their last legs, and K-mart quality fins. That sure wasn't the case with Luis and Jose. Their equipment was as new and as modern as my gear. I even was envious of the two Longines Hydroquest dive watches they wore, which easily cost over a thousand dollars each. Jose looked at me ogling over the gear and explained. "Gringos come to Acapulco with fat wallets and lots of time. Some come to drink, some for the señoritas," (He cast a sidelong glance at my dad). Some to get *on* the water for bill fishing, and some get *in* the water." He added with a smile, "We consider it our national duty to make those wallets thinner." While we got our gear in order, the *Saturday* hovered over the first 'hit," lowered her mailbox blowers, and started clearing overburden. After the silt cleared, we went below to the internal dive platform in the crew quarters. Before heading below decks, we checked out the two-way radios and I peered out on the water for any unwelcome fins.

"Are you sure your pet shark is far away?" I asked David.

"She's long gone." He answered, and then with a smirk, added, "Unless she's got an untagged sister or boyfriend in the neighborhood!"

"Understand," I said. "I'm dumb but not stupid. I'm not afraid to dive when there are sharks in the water. I've done it a hundred times, but nobody wants to play chicken with that dental work."

Luis, overhearing my concerns, peered out at the smooth seas. "Tiburon?" he asked nervously. It was obvious he didn't want to join the food chain any more than I did.

I tried to sound casual. "Nothing in sight," I said, as calm as possible. "But Bric will keep an eye out and let us know if we have company."

Coming into the crew cabin, Bric announced to the three of us, "Gentlemen, the stage is yours! Diver-down time!" Finally, after so many weeks, we were actually going to play in the water.

I took a few quick test breaths on the BC, picked up the portable metal detector with one hand, grabbed the bar above the dive ladder, and swung into the bathtub-warm water. The sand and silt had cleared from the mailbox blower work and I could see the unmistakable outline of at least two encrusted cannons. The whole area was also scattered with pieces of porcelain, either broken during the wreck or blown to smithereens by the powerful wash of the mailboxes. I reported my observations by radio as I swam toward the bottom in the crystal clear water. We hadn't reached the bottom when we were surrounded by curious seals swooping and playing in front of us. I was happy to have the company. As long as the seals hung around, bad guys with teeth wouldn't be.

Eager to find a bunch of silver, I got to the bottom and started poking around. Luis and Jose joined me a minute later. David had upgraded our gear since our Haitian adventure to a set of AqualPulse AQ1B metal detectors, the choice of just about every treasure boat in the water, since our Haitian adventure. The detector started squealing in my ear even before I got to the bottom.

"Drop a basket!" I called into the built-in mic. Dad didn't even bother to answer me as a metal basket on thin line settled a few feet away. I didn't immediately find a pile of silver or gold – that would have been too easy. I did pick up some encrusted objects and dropped them in the basket, along with a stack of blue-painted porcelain cups, so perfect that looked like they had been put there yesterday. I guessed the silt had kept those cups covered since shortly after the ship sunk and were exposed when the mailboxes blew, so there wasn't any encrustation. My metal detector kept screaming in my ear, but aside from the huge cannon, there wasn't a lot to gather from the hole. I looked at Luis and Jose. They both put thumbs-down. No treasure. I jerked the line twice, signaling Bric to pull up the basket, and pointed to Luis and Jose to head back to the *Saturday*.

Dad was waiting at the head of the dive ladder and took our fins so we could climb up the stairs. By the time we showered the salt water off our bodies and rinsed our gear in fresh, David had sorted the basket contents and had the encrusted pieces soaking in a solution. I could tell by his frown something worried him.

"All these cups and pottery you found concern me," he said. "I would have expected the cargo from Asia would have been unloaded in Acapulco. Well, maybe it was destined for Panama." Brightening up, he added, "I think this is just the beginning of a debris field. Anything of real value would have been secured well below, and won't be found until we find the main wreck. I'll send FRED back up to follow the debris."

"Ah, I don't know how valuable that porcelain is," I said. "But you might be a little gentler with the blowers. I think it was turning dishes into porcelain confetti."

David flared a bit. "Do you want to stock your china cupboard or fill your pockets? Sure that stuff has value, but one silver bar would buy half a truckload of old China cups." He waggled a finger to stress his point. "Focus! Keep your eye on the prize."

This went on for several days, marking a 'hit', blowing the overburden off, diving the hole, and never finding much of significance, other than some encrusted metal, a few cannons that we photographed and left in place, lots of porcelain pieces and one wooden chunk that had been buried in the silt. I put it in the basket, mostly because I was surprised that anything wood would have lasted this long.

Topside after the dive, I found David and my dad admiring it. When they washed it in a tub, you could see it was a large piece of black wood and was pierced with three large holes. "It's a deadeye," Dad announced.

"Dead what?" I asked.

"Deadeye," he answered. "It's part of the ship's rigging and was used to secure the mast. This piece lasted this long because it was buried in silt soon after sinking, and it's probably made from ironwood, hard as steel. In the Pacific, they used the wood from the Lignum Vitae tree, which is almost as hard."

After a half dozen mailbox blows and dry runs, it became evident the *Leon* spilled its guts for miles. "The Atocha did the same thing," Dad reminded us. "But it came apart in a hurricane, and another storm scattered the main pile even further. I'm starting to believe that's what sunk this ship. We've got better equipment than Mel Fisher had back then, but this could still take quite a while."

"The scatter appears to be in one line," David pointed out. "I think we will find the main part of the wreck sooner than later."

It became routine. FRED would get a new hit, we would stop, blow the area with the mailboxes, wait for the water to clear, then the three of us would go down for a look-see. The water was bathtub-warm, and none of us bothered with wetsuits. I believe a wetsuit makes you look like a seal in the eyes of a white shark and increases your chance of entering the food chain. Regardless, I'm proud of my lily-white body today.

Our first clue on this dive was the sudden disappearance of the ever-present sea lions. They were conspicuous by their absence. A few seconds later, Bric's voice squawked on my radio, "We've got company, Brody, a hundred yards off the port bow. I think your girlfriend's back. I would guess she would love to have you over for dinner." I looked up at the *Saturday*, saw which way the bow was pointing, and peered into the distance for any menacing shape. Luis and Jose weren't wearing radios, so I pulled my dive knife out of the sheath on my calf and tapped my aluminum air tank sharply three times. Sound travels better in water than land and both divers looked my way. I pointed in the direction my dad said Dolly was coming from and put my hand above my head, simulating a shark fin. White sharks attack by ambush, coming from below at speed to knock their prey, seals, penguins (or humans). I knew our best defense was to hug the bottom until she was out of sight. Luis and Jose obviously had some experience or training, as they stayed quietly on the bottom, making no motion. I had slightly negative weight in my belt so I didn't struggle to keep myself on the bottom while I was looking for loot, so I just rolled on my back, and lay in the hole made by the blowers, and waited. A minute later, a shadow passed between me and the yacht. From where I was, it looked like a 747 with pectoral fins, cruising by. I took a breath from my regulator and held it. I'm good anytime for three minutes underwater without breathing, a bad habit if you're going up or down with scuba gear, but perfectly safe if you are not moving. I think Luis and Jose caught on, and the three of us lay on the bottom without making bubbles until the shape moved out of sight. We took a few breaths when she slid into the distance, then clamped down again as the shark cruised back by, before turning toward the shore to see if there were any seal stragglers. We waited five more minutes, still and quiet as mice, before dad radioed me. "It looks like the coast is clear," he said, obviously relieved. "I can see the dorsal fin nearly a quarter-mile toward shore." He tried to sound relaxed when he added, "You might want to come up for milk and cookies."

And change my shorts.

It was quite a bit later, after almost another month of dry holes before the MagArrow marked a huge magnetic anomaly. "I think we've found her," David announced. "Let me position the *Saturday* and start blowing."

We waited again for the silt to clear, and dropped down with our metal detectors, expecting to find a mountain of silver on the bottom. Even from fifty feet above, Luis exclaimed, "This is the place! I recognize that outcropping, and there's the anchor just past those three cannons!"

But no silver or gold. I assumed we blew the wrong spot, so after a brief look, I signaled for us to head back aboard so the *Saturday* could reposition. Before we did go to the surface, I did see something interesting, some large, smooth yellowish blocks of some sort, with the initials "PR" in large raised script cast on the side. I would guess them at about thirty pounds each. I picked up a couple and dropped them in the basket, jerking on the rope to signal dad to pull it up.

By the time we got to the surface, stowed our gear, and came out on deck, David was sitting on a stool and staring at the blocks with the most dejected look I've ever seen.

"Who shot your puppy?" I asked.

"We're done here," he answered with a frown. "Stow your gear. We're heading back to port."

"But we're not done down there," I answered, not understanding. "There's a whole lot of wreck that is still covered with overburden. What makes you so sure it's an empty wreck?" I was asking for the four of us, my dad, Luis, Jose, and me.

He looked up at us and answered with a single word.

"Beeswax."

Wayne Gales

12

"Beeswax?" I asked. "That's what those blocks of yellow stuff are?"

"Yes, I'm sad to say," David answered glumly, digging at one of the blocks with a pocket knife. "I was already getting concerned with all the porcelain scattered about, but when you brought up two blocks of beeswax, I knew that, regardless of this wreck being in the wrong place, it had *definitely* not made port in Acapulco. She won't have any silver or gold on her." Standing up, he folded the knife and brushed his hands with finality. "Time to cut our losses and go home." Keying his walkie-talkie, he spoke, "Captain Novak, stow the mailbox blowers, weigh the anchors and head back to port. This party's over." Novak didn't question the order, and just responded with a crisp "Aye-aye."

I wasn't totally satisfied with the answer, other than being disappointed that this was another dry hole. "What did they use beeswax for, and what's the 'PR' insignia on the side? Any significance or value?"

"Well, it probably confirms this was the *San Marcos de Leon,*" David answered. "The 'PR' stands for Philip Rey, Phillip the Fifth, or Philippe, Duc d'Anjou, King of Spain from 1700 until he died in 1746. They would have put his chop on everything he owned. The *Leon* went missing in 1745 so this is pretty well positive evidence that we have found it. Beeswax," David explained, "was strictly for use in the new world. It burned much cleaner than the smelly and smoky tallow candles made from animal fat."

"Shouldn't we donate the blocks to a museum or something?" I asked. "I'm sure they would welcome it."

David held up a hand, signaling caution. "You forget we aren't supposed to be here. Unless you are into candle making, we might as well toss them back." David brightened a little. "Maybe we could give our politician friends a heads-up so they can 'discover' the site and get it under the UNESCO umbrella."

Luis sort of shuffled his feet at that suggestion. "Ah, Señor David, por favor, could you maybe wait a month or two before providing that information so we can collect a few items? Rich

Gringas will pay a fortune for an old China cup on el *Mercado Negro*, the black market." With a smile, he added, "That's how we make a living. Since you have done such a good job with the mailbox blowers, we can sneak out here after you leave, go diving for *langostas,* and accidentally find some pottery lying on the bottom." David looked toward dad and me as if we had a vote in this request. I nodded vigorously. Luis and Jose had become trusted friends in just a few weeks.

We motored back to the yacht harbor in silence, disappointed the *Leon* had been carrying no treasure. "As I've said before," Bricreminded me with a hand on my shoulder. "That's why they call it treasure hunting." When we tied up to the dock and started our farewell wishes to our new friends, I suddenly had an inspiration.

"Hey, do you guys have passports?" Dad looked at me, and quickly nodded approval when he figured out why I asked. "Si, Señor Brody, Jose and I go to San Francisco at least once a year to visit our seester," Luis answered. I suspected he guessed where this was leading to. Pointing to the ship next to us. I asked, "How would the two of you like to help us crew the *Seaglass* back to Key West, in exchange for a plane ticket back home, or wherever you want to go?" I added as an afterthought, "It's just Dad, the cook, and me on the boat. We got here that way, and it's doable, just a little much for the two of us on such a long trip. We would appreciate the help." The two brothers stepped away from us and spoke quietly in Spanish to each other for a minute. They seemed to agree and walked back toward my father and me. With a smile, Luis answered. He was usually the spokesperson for the duo. "Si, Señor Brody, we will join your crew." Looking at the *Seaglass*, he added with some concern. "We've never sailed on such a large yacht. How is she to handle?"

With a smile, I answered, "She almost sails herself. Just follow the compass and dodge the occasional island while we catch a nap. Piece of cake."

We shook hands all around and walked over to *Seaglass*. Cookie was still sitting at the top of the gangway just like we left him, arms folded with his meat cleaver in hand. He stood and welcomed us back aboard with a big smile. Looking with expectation, he asked, "Treasure?"

"Not this time," Dad answered. Reaching in his backpack he pulled out a porcelain cup. "Unless you call this treasure. Authentic Ming dynasty from the seventeenth century. I thought you might like it. Most of the china we found was Ching dynasty, but we found some of these too." Cookie dropped the cleaver on the deck, narrowly missing lopping off his big toe. Taking the cup in both hands, he fell to his knees, and then stood and bowed deeply from the waist, looking up at Bric with tears in his eyes. "My ancestors were poor farmers in China since the fourteenth century during the Ming Dynasty. We would have never been fortunate enough to possess such a cup. I am honored, Mr. Bric, to accept this gift. I shall cherish it."

"Oh, don't go getting mushy on me, Cookie," Dad answered with a wave. "It's just a cup Brody pulled up from a wreck. It was one of the only things we found with any value."

"It's priceless to me," Cookie answered. Bowing again, he picked up the cleaver and retreated to his quarters.

"Let me show you around," I motioned to the two Mexicans. Luis answered again. "señor Brody, we need to go back home and get a few items, including our passports, and we also need to say goodbye to a few friends so they won't worry." Dad answered for both of us with a sly smile, "Make it three days, call it Saturday by noon. I've, ah, got a little unfinished business to attend to."

"I guess that leaves me to get *Seaglass* ready to sail," I said with a sigh.

"Mister Brody," Cookie had come back from his cabin and touched me on the arm. "I took the liberty of using your Amex card to get her ready for the voyage home." He counted off on his fingers. "Fuel, food, bottled water, and," nodding toward my dad with a little distaste, "Rum." Bowing even deeper, he added, "I apologize if you do not approve of my purchases."

All I could do was laugh. "No, Cookie, you did just fine. I guess all I have to do is find that *Fonda* for dinner again."

"We'll join you!" Luis and Jose said in one voice, sniffing the opportunity for a free meal. "Meet there at seven for La Ultima Cena, the last supper in Acapulco!"

I frowned at that. It sounded more like a prophecy than a farewell.

Wayne Gales

13
Flashback

The *San Marcos de Leon* was in dire peril. Almost every single member of the crew lay dead or dying from various ailments. They had long since abandoned the task of climbing the rigging to adjust, furl, or deploy the sails, for fear of falling to their death from weakness on the rolling deck. The captain of the galleon and the first lieutenant had succumbed that morning to malaria, hastened by scurvy and starvation. The ship's master pilot laid delirious, leaving his apprentice, Francisco, no more than fifteen years old, and the cabin boy, Dinero, who had always taken his meals with the Asian contingent, hardly more than ten, as the only two people aboard capable of movement. Both stood at the huge wheel trying to pilot the lumbering galleon. They were aware the ship had overshot the harbor entrance and feared the consequences in Acapulco should they make a mistake.

The few crew members and soldiers still alive languished on the deck or below, the gun ports, normally latched well down unless a threat was near, were all thrown open to provide a little fresh air and to combat the fetid smell.

The bulky, square-sailed galleons of the day might have been state of the art in eighteenth-century sailing vessels, but were awkward and clumsy, and nearly impossible to sail into a headwind. The art of tacking, sailing in a zig-zag motion to get to an upwind destination required exceptional piloting skills, well beyond the ability of the boys, one an apprentice and the other a mere child.

Looking past the stern of the *Leon*, Francisco watched the familiar mouth of his boyhood home, Acapulco harbor, growing smaller by the minute.

"Giro de Vuelta!" cried the cabin boy. "Turn around!" pulling hard on one side of the massive wheel. While responding easily to slight course corrections, a drastic turn took more effort. Reaching high on the wheel until his small body was completely off the ground while the other child pushed up as hard as he could

97

on the other side, the helm slowly responded, turning the lumbering galleon to the left.

Different than the vision of a man-o-war of the day, bristling with over a hundred cannon, arranged through three decks, Manila galleons had a single gun deck, located just below the man deck. The gun ports were high on the side of the ship, but not high enough to avoid what followed next.

What followed was predictable and tragic. Any competent pilot would never make a drastic course change in a brisk wind without reefing all but a few of the galleon's sails, but the apprentice had never been taught such a maneuver. As the mighty ship slowly turned broadside to the brisk wind, the broad sails caught and made the big ship lurch dangerously to one side, causing bodies, sick sailors, and soldiers below to be tossed to the far side of the hull. Despite the ship heeling so far over, she might have survived the turn had the gun ports not been tied open, instantly flooding the lower deck. The weight of the water, the huge cannon, some weighing over two tons each crashed across the deck, crushing the few living crewmen with a scream and punching through the thick hull, dealing the *Leon* a mortal blow.

The ship was doomed. Having survived months at sea, burdened with malnutrition, scurvy, and malaria, the *San Marcos de Leon* rolled on her side scattering cannons and merchandise along the bottom for several miles. Her precious cargo of silks, porcelain, spices, and a fortune in other valuable merchandise was rendered worthless as they settled to the bottom for eternity, only a few miles from her destination. A small herd of sea lions, having established a nursery on a nearby beach for millennia, curiously frolicked around the wreckage and bodies, slowly descending toward the nearby bottom.

Dinero may have been the youngest member of the crew, but he had an advantage over everybody else on the ship. Growing up on the streets, klongs, and rivers of Krung Thep, Dinero could swim almost as soon as he could walk.

As the ship rolled, tossing Francisco and Dinero into the ocean, the young boy watched his friend thrash on the surface for a few moments before sliding beneath the waves. Striking out for shore in comfortable strides, he was spared from the gathering pelagic predators as they feasted on the doomed sailors, the only surviving member of the crew. The *Leon* slowly sunk below the waves at twilight, with only the vacant eyes of the dead, a dozen playful seals, and one little boy to witness her settle to the bottom, where she began a slow disintegration, to be untouched for more than three hundred and fifty years.

14

Luis and Jose walked down the dock the morning after, "No dive gear?" I pointed at the small backpack each was carrying. Luis laughed, "We have spent our whole lives in or under the water. It's time for a real *vacacion*. Besides," he added, "It's muy *dificil* to drag all that gear on an airplane when we go home."

As for my dad, it wasn't three days, but five, before Pop showed up, looking over his shoulder and using any available cover as he walked shirtless and barefoot into the yacht harbor. When he got to *Seaglass* he gave me an upside-down salute with his left hand. He laughed, "Permission to come aboard, Captain!"

"What did you do, rob a bank?" I asked sarcastically. Looking over his shoulder again, he explained, "How did I know? She was sitting in a bar, looking sad and drinking tequila shots out of a porcelain cup. I just sat down and volunteered comfort, and didn't find out until five shots and one worm later she was the mayor's wife!" He rolled his eyes, "Next thing I know, somebody's kicking a hotel door down and I'm throwing my shorts out of the window. I climbed down the second-floor fire escape buck naked." Smiling he added, "I'm glad the Alcalde and his boys were bad shots!" He made like he was mopping his brow. "Whew! That was a close one!" Looking toward town one more time with a worried glance, he suggested, "Perhaps we could set sail sooner than later?"

Easier said than done. I warmed up the twin diesels, showed Luis and Jose how to cast off the lines fore and aft, and radioed the harbormaster we were departing. It took a good fifteen minutes to get underway, and Bric beat a strategic retreat below decks and out of sight. He came up and breathed a sigh of relief when we finally sailed out of Acapulco Harbor. "Maybe you've learned a lesson," I suggested.

"At seventy, if I haven't learned by now," Dad answered with a sly smile, "I probably never will."

It only took a few days before we dropped into a routine. Life was much easier with a four-man crew, especially while we were on open seas. Although the brothers didn't have any big-boat experience, they both had been aboard sailboats since they were teenagers and had enough basic skills to let dad and me catch some decent naps throughout the day. We were still up and alert at night, while the Mexicans got their sleep.

As much as we needed to be on duty at night to make sure the *Seaglass* didn't run into some unexpected reef or ship coming from the Panama Canal, we had an equally important reason. My father and I share a love for a night sky in the middle of an ocean unpolluted by light, a treat few people ever get to experience. I was barely more than six years old when my dad took me out in the gulf one night, far from Key West lights, and infected me with a love of the stars that I'll never lose. We didn't pay much attention to the stars on the way to Mexico. I guess we were too focused on getting there, but on the way home, we were in a different frame of mind. The first night we were clear of any nearby ships, we shut off every light on the yacht and took in the planets, stars, the Milky Way, which looked more like a cloud than a band of stars, and even distant galaxies, each with billions of suns. "At night in a city, even in the suburbs without a lot of light pollution, you can pick out a few hundred stars, maybe four planets, and a couple of the more visible constellations, like the big dipper and Orion," Dad noted one night. "Out here you can see over forty thousand with the naked eye. And," he added, "If you know where to look, you can see nine galaxies and thirteen nebulae. This time of year, my old friends, Cygnus, Bootes, Hercules, and as always, the Ursa Major, the Big Dipper." Motioning toward the north, he said. "Draw a straight line from the end of the Dipper's cup, and there's Polaris, the Pole star, pointing true North, helping seafarers find their way since man first sailed a boat in the sea millennia ago."

Looking up, I asked him to show me something I already knew how to find. It just pleased him every time, so I asked anyway. "Show me a galaxy."

Being mid-summer, dad knew right where to look. It was only a few hours after sunset, and he pointed east, well above the horizon. "It's easy." He started, "First you find Cassiopeia. It looks like a big 'W', there. The second star from the top is Schedar. Now, look a little way down and to the right. See that fuzzy looking star?" I could almost see him smile in the dark. "That's Andromeda. Our nearest neighbor. Two and a half million light-years away, and over a trillion stars." He continued, back in his 'teacher' mode. "If you could travel at light speed, a feat that's very unlikely unless your name is Han Solo or Captian Kirk, it would take you far longer to reach it than man has existed on this earth as Homo Sapiens." He sounded a little sad then, "We better learn to take better care of this rock pretty soon. It's not like we can sail off to a different planet." And he drifted off in deep thought.

It made me think, too.

Days later we stopped again in Panama City for supplies and a little sightseeing, but the boys decided not to get off. "No need to go through passport control and get visas," explained Luis, almost cryptically.

Hmm, that was a little strange. As long as they stayed on board, Luis and Jose could transit the canal zone without being checked. After passing Gatun Locks, we stopped again a day later in Colon to refuel. Again, the Mexicans declined to get off the *Seaglass*. "You see one Latin town, you've seen them all," Luis answered with a stretch and a yawn. We had a pet Labrador retriever when I was growing up, and he always yawned when something made him nervous. Strange, very strange.

As soon as we were in cell phone range, I called Mallory, having not talked to her since we left Key West. "I have a little surprise," she said. I could visualize her smile over the phone. "I've decided to take a little sabbatical from my studies. I'll be home next week." I was overjoyed with this news. "That's great!" I answered, "But why the change in plans?" Her answer was almost cryptic. She even giggled a little. "Because I miss your face, and it's time to play house for a while and stuff."

Stuff? This totally confused me. Mallory is loving, kind, sincere, and caring, but I've never seen her joke or kid much from the time we first met. When I told her once that I loved her for her mind. She dryly answered that I probably wouldn't cross the street to attend a wet hat contest.

She had a point there.

I also called ahead to arrange a new berth in Key West Harbor. It was a longer ride to my houseboat than her old berth for Mal and me, but I knew she couldn't fit anywhere in Garrison Bight. It was a bit farther for my dad too, but it didn't look like we planned any more adventures at the moment. When we approached our new slip, Luis and Jose staged themselves like we trained, one at the bow and the other brother on the stern, tossing lines to a shore crew as we idled up. Nobody was there to officially welcome us back. even though we had been away for a few months. The *Seaglass* was familiar in the town, and with Key West as an official home base, I think they just assumed we had not gone far. Once we tied up and got the big yacht powered down and secured, I piled my gear on the dock to take back to the houseboat. Dad left with what he came with, a little backpack, a change of clothes, a hat, and his spare pair of flip-flops since he abandoned the others on some hotel room floor in Acapulco. Cookie lived aboard so there was no need to button her up completely. I couldn't help but notice that Luis and Jose had retreated below deck when we docked. Dad followed me down the stairs into the cabin where the brothers were sitting, bags in hand. "Not in a hurry to experience Key West?" I asked

"No, Señor Brody," Jose answered this time. They looked at each other, embarrassed, obviously wanting to tell me something. I sat on a stool in front of them for a minute, waiting for someone to talk, then finally broke the silence. "Let me guess, you aren't in a hurry to run down the dock for the same reason you didn't want to visit Panama." I looked at both brothers, one at a time with my hands on my hips, as sternly as a twenty seven year old could look at two seniors. "You don't have passports."

They both suddenly seemed to take great interest in their toenails. After a minute Luis finally spoke. With a quiet voice, he confessed. "Señor Brody, you are correct. We have never been to Los Estados Unidos. We have applied for work visas, for *passaportas*, even for political asylum over the years, but never with success." Looking up, there was hope in his eyes. "When you asked us to join you on the trip home as crew, we saw free passage to America, far from any Mexico border. We have enough dinero, plus the money you promised us, to get to our sister in San Francisco." He finished with an apology. "Señor Brody, *lo siento*, we are sorry we deceived you, but you would never have risked going to jail if you had been caught with illegal aliens."

I was getting a little hot under the collar at the risk they had put us in, but when I looked toward my dad, he was starting to smile. "Well, as they say, that's agua under the bridge. We're here and nobody's in prison. I can't blame you for wanting to live in this country," he chuckled. "If, for no other reason, we have colder *cerveza* and better roads." Looking toward me, he added. "Brody promised you airfare back to Acapulco. I'm sure he's willing to give you cash. How soon do you plan to head west?"

Relieved they weren't going to be turned in, Luis, as always, answered for his brother. "We have heard much about Key West and Florida. We would like to hang around for a few weeks, then go to Orlando and visit El Ratoncito, the mouse as you call it. Can you recommend an inexpensive place on this island that we can rent for a few weeks?"

It was my turn to laugh. "The words 'Key West' and 'inexpensive' aren't used together very often. You will pay more in a week here for a room than a Mexican citizen would pay in a month, or two for a whole apartment." I looked at my dad for suggestions.

"I have an idea," he said. "You two can stay at my apartment behind Hunks. I'll just hang out at my hideaway on Geiger Key."

I ran the three of them over to the apartment in my Jeep, where Bric showed them where the key was hidden and introduced them to Kevin. "They are my guests for a few weeks," he explained to the bar owner. "They are welcome to stay as long as they wish." We said our goodbyes and my dad got in his POS Toyota for the trip home. I hugged him goodbye and reflected before he left. "Well, that trip was a waste," I said before he backed out of the garage.

"Speak for yourself," Dad answered. "It's been a while since I've been off the leash and off the island at the same time." He stretched his arms. "I don't consider that voyage was a waste at all." He added with a sly smile, "When it's good it's great, and when it's bad, it's still great."

15

A week later, Mal walked out of the Key West Terminal towing her familiar rollaboard. Mallory Cohen is one of the few women I've ever known who could pack her entire life in a suitcase that could fit in an airline overhead bin. She was wearing shorts and a tank top and walked in strappy leather sandals, her arms and legs still honey-colored as if she left yesterday.

"Is that normal attire for England?" I asked in the middle of a bear hug and hello kiss.

"My flat in Cambridge had a roof access," she explained. "The other girls and I learned to lay out there on any sunny day without classes. We always locked the door so we could get an even tan, if you get my drift until airplanes on approach got wind of it and changed their landing pattern." She added with a laugh. "We called that roof South Beach."

I picked up her luggage, took her by the arm, and guided her toward the Jeep. She turned toward me before climbing in. Punching me in the gut with a finger, she exclaimed, "We go back on our training program tomorrow morning. So, prepare for a proper ass-kicking just after sunrise. Self-defense training, round two, only a little more serious this time." She looked sternly at my boyish figure. "Looks like you fell off the wagon a little on your adventure with my brother. I hope you enjoyed your little holiday. Starting today, both of us start getting back in shape."

Looking her up and down, I didn't see a single inch that wasn't 'in shape'. "Can't we wait until tomorrow morning?" I groaned. There's a Mexican restaurant on Stock Island that I've been dying to go back to. I've developed a new appetite for Latin food. Dad says they have the world's best fajitas."

"We can go tonight," she said with a stern look. "But I'll bet they have some nice salads on the menu also."

So, this is Hell.

As she promised, our training regimen started up the next morning, running, exercising, and sparing. The tutoring each night made my high school days feel like Sesame Street. Mal accessorized our training with some fitness training items, courtesy of my credit card and shipping from Amazon. In a few days, a full-size B.O.B punching dummy arrived via the Amazon Prime truck, among some other stuff. After clearing all the furniture in the living room of our houseboat and cramming it into the spare bedroom, we turned it into a real live training camp. Mallory was brutal to BOB and had little trouble kicking him time after time in the head, neck, torso, and imaginary crotch. I think Mallory's Mossad training was even more brutal than what my dad learned with the SEALS. I feel sorry for any guy who ever met her in a dark alley with impure things on his mind. He's probably still looking for his package.

Despite falling off the diet during our voyage to Mexico, it only took a week or so before I could keep up with her during our morning runs. Mal whipped me back into shape in short order but I doubt I'll ever be as violent as she is.

That's just not Brody Wahl.

In six weeks, Mal changed me in ways I never thought possible. I mean I have never been considered dumb, and I've always been a whiz at math when it counted. But Mal got me to butch up on reading and writing and showed me that the Sunday Key West Citizen was useful for more than just wrapping mackerel. She also taught me that there was a life beyond cheeseburgers. I always thought up to now that green things weren't food, but what food eats. Between straightening out my diet, morning runs, and a brutal exercise program, my six foot three, two hundred and sixty-pound body has been converted into a svelte two-oh-five.

And she taught me the meaning of the word, svelte.

Oh, the fitness regimen wasn't non-stop. At least once, or maybe twice a week, if I could talk her into it, we went up to Geiger Key, borrowed Dad's twenty-foot Key West center console, and headed either out in the gulf for dolphin or into Florida Bay for some hefty permit and cobia. Our favorite spot was over the World War Two wreck Edward Luckenbach, sunk in fifty-five feet of water in the Florida Straits in 1942 when she strayed off course and and struck an American mine. Permit are a sleek, disc-shaped fish, a distant relative of pompano and tuna, and a hoot to catch. You put a little crab on your hook and take your line toward the bottom, moving the boat away from the wreck site when (and if) you hook up. Permit are wide and flat, and if you nail a twenty-pounder, it feels like you have a runaway F-16 on the end of the line. They turn sideways and fight like hell. I've caught many, ranging from fifteen pounds to a thirty-five-pound whopper. They taste great, broiled, or on the grill, but nowadays we always let them go to help preserve this threatened species.

After fishing, we loved to park on the natural sandy beach at Snipe Point for sun and relaxation. Marvin Key is nicer, but fond memories of the good times with my dad and his friend Rumpy, rest his soul, soaking in the bathtub warm waters, munching Key West Pink Shrimp make visits to there too painful.

One morning after our workout, Mallory announced, "Get in the shower and blow the stink off. We're going on a power shop."

I could think of a dozen things I'd rather do than go shopping on Duval Street, like fishing, diving, or looking for treasure.

"I'd love to honey, but I've got a root canal scheduled for this morning."

"That's news to me," she answered looking skeptical. "When was this planned?"

I pulled my cell phone out of my pocket. "As soon as I call the dentist," I answered.

For some strange reason, she wouldn't take no for an answer and I found myself trudging from store to store in Old Town, trying to look interested while she held dress after dress in front of her, asking my opinion as if my taste was anything of value. After two hours, I pointed out, "Mallory, you don't wear anything around this town but shorts and a tank top, or maybe a khaki dress. What's the sudden change in wardrobe to Mother Hubbard floral dresses?" She smiled but didn't answer and dragged me to five more stores in the next two hours. That root canal was starting to look like a more and more promising alternative. I resigned myself to a day of endless clothing shops.

Ignoring my gripe, she held up yet another dress up for my approval, I finally admitted, "Honestly, Mal, I can't tell one from the other."

"I like this one," she said with confidence. Finally, I thought to myself, and then observed, "It's nice, but isn't it a little big for you?"

Her answer didn't make sense, at least for a moment.

Her eyes were almost twinkling when she answered, "Oh, I'll grow into it in a few months."

"I thought both of us were on strict...wait a minute. YOU'RE PREGNANT?"

I guess I was a little loud. Everyone in the store froze and turned our way. "Could you speak up?" Mallory said, laughing, "I don't think that sleeping drunk we saw on the curb across from the Pier House quite heard you." Still smiling, she confirmed, "Yes, barely two months now, from my calculations. I peed on a stick this morning to make sure. It was positive!" I hugged her, kissed her, and started to swing her around by the waist, then stopped. "Uh in your condition, I guess I better be a little gentler."

"I'm pregnant, not turned to glass," she said with a smile. "I spoke to the OBGYN this morning and he said that anything I did before, I can do now. Oh, no more diving after four months, and our hand-to-hand practice will have to become a little gentler soon," she smiled again, "Not that you've ever been able to hit me."

That reminder prompted me to change the subject. "What are we going to name the little alien?" I asked. "When they are born, they all look like aliens."

Mallory was slow to answer. "I've had a name in my mind since I was a little girl, dreaming of the time I would have my own little one. Our family has a tradition that we name our children after ancestors, but my father named me Mallory after his favorite place in the world, Mallory Square. Someplace he used to hang out with his drinking buddy." Stabbing me in the chest, she surprised me with a revelation, "Your father." Wow, I knew my dad knew Mallory's father, and taught him how to dive, but I never knew they were close friends. I wish I had met him. It made me love her a little more.

If that's possible.

Mallory continued. "My middle name was a recognition of my grandmother on my mother's side, Elizabeth. If we have a girl, she will be Abigail Elizabeth."

"I've never heard you speak of your grandmother. Was she from Israel?"

Mallory looked wistful, a tear in her eye. "I never knew her, but many stories have been told. She was in the Israeli Army in 1967 and was defending a position on the Golan Heights with a company of men and women. History says our air force took out the Arab planes before they could strike, but at least one jet got through to their location. A MiG17 strafed the Israeli position at low altitude. Grandma and several other soldiers emptied their Uzis into the MiG, but the strafing killed her and eight others in her squad when it passed over." She looked at me through her tears. "Legend has it her Uzi connected, and the MiG never regained altitude, crashing into the desert a short distance away. There is a plaque in a cemetery in Jerusalem in their honor."

"Wow," I remarked. "You must get that fighting talent from her."

Smiling grimly, she replied. "You have no idea."

"That takes care of a girl's name." I pointed out, "What if it's a boy?"

"Then you name him," she answered, with a sniff. "And we'll keep trying until we get a girl."

Wayne Gales

16

Grandpa and Grandma Cohen were apparently just fine with Mallory and me living in sin on the houseboat, but when we visited the senior home in Miami to let them know they were going to be great-grandparents, their demeanor changed in a New York minute. "Time to make this official," Golda, sitting up in her wheelchair, said with authority. "Moishe, I'll get in touch with Goodman and let him know what mischief his goddaughter has been up to. I'll be sure to tell him that we're pleased with the developments so he doesn't do something rash and assure him we know and we approve of her choice, but it's time we seal the deal. I'm sure Mr. Goodman will be more than happy to make the arrangements."

As we drove back to Key West, I acted excited while I was terrified inwardly, conjuring up visions of a massive ceremony in a big temple someplace in New York with a thousand guests, limousines, and bodyguards.

As it turned out, that was far from the real plans. Unlike Moishe, who never talked on the phone, (which is why we had to pay a personal visit) I got a call a few days later from a cold, impersonal, curt, female voice. Without a hello, introduction, or go fly a kite, she announced, "Hold for Mr. Goodman." The weak voice of an old man came on the line. I sat the phone on the table and put it on speaker so Mal could hear both ends of the conversation. "Well, Broderick," Goodman started without any chit-chat, "I understand you have committed an indiscretion with my goddaughter." Caught a little off guard with his using my full name, I started stammering an explanation that, while the baby was not exactly planned, but welcomed, he interrupted me. "It's perfectly understandable, young man. I have known her since she sat on my lap, with a wet kiss on one end and a wet diaper on the other. Mallory has never been a slave to convention, but people of our faith always make this union official as soon as possible, and legal." I breathed a sigh of relief at his approval. I didn't want to end up trying to swim across Florida Bay with cinder blocks tied around my feet. "Leave the arrangements to Moishe, Golda, and me." There was a little pause. "I apologize in advance to Mallory that my desire to stay out of the public eye these days will mandate the event be in a rather discrete location. You may bring your father, Broderick, and I'm sure Mallory will wish to select a maid of honor. Just make sure it's a trusted person."

Mal hesitated for a moment in thought, then brightened. "Brody's half-sister, Mary Beth. I haven't asked her, but I'm sure she would love to be there."

"Excellent," he answered. "Broderick, let me make a few calls and I will be in touch soon with plans." He hung up without another word. Mallory was beaming with approval at the plans. It was obvious she had no more interest in a huge formal ceremony than I did.

I would guess if dad had called Mary Beth for any reason, she might have turned him down, but she welcomed the call from Mal and happily agreed to stand with her at the ceremony. Now, all we had to do was wait.

We didn't hear a peep for a few weeks, and then got another rather cryptic call from Mr. Goodman's secretary and assistant, Gloria. "Billy will pick up Mallory, your sister, your father, and you next Saturday morning in the Gulfstream. Sorry, but no other guests will be permitted, per Mr. Goodman."

Before she could hang up, I had a few questions. "Gloria, we haven't had time to rent tuxes, and Mal doesn't have a wedding dress (even though it wouldn't be white). What do we wear?" I could tell Gloria covered the mouthpiece with her hand while she consulted. "I'm sorry, Brody, I don't have all the plans myself. Mr. Goodman advised this would be a very casual wedding in a tropical setting. Shorts are appropriate and Mr. Goodman will bring his synagogue's Rabbi for the ceremony. The services will be performed with the acknowledgment of those present, and the eyes of God but not necessarily by the state of Florida. He also suggests you have a civil ceremony in Key West at your convenience to make it legal in Florida." And she hung up.

Curiouser and Curiouser.

At Gloria's direction, a few days later we all gathered at the Monroe County Courthouse and waded through all the paperwork for a civil ceremony. We filled out the forms, paid our $93.50, and twenty minutes later, we were standing in front of the Clerk of Courts. Everything went smoothly until I was instructed to put the ring on her finger. "I forgot the ring! Everybody wait here! I'll be right back!" Before I could turn to run, Mallory took my arm. "Woah, there, Cowboy. If I let you leave, we might not see you again until after lobster season." With a smile, she reached into a pocket and pulled out a familiar black sock. I looked at it with astonishment. "The last time I saw that it was in a drawer in a dresser, in a storage unit behind Searstown. How did you know?" Mallory tipped the sock upside down and Dad's diamond ring tumbled into her hand. "Sometimes you talk in your sleep," she answered. "Sometimes I listen. I knew right where to look."

With a sheepish grin, I took the ring and slipped it on her finger. I didn't even hear the clerk say, "By the power vested in me by the State of Florida, I pronounce you man and wife." With a smile, she finished, "You may kiss the bride."

I heard that part.

Billy, Goodman's private pilot, called us from New York Saturday morning. "Wheels up on this end after we get fueled and stocked with beverages. We should be in Key West in about three hours. I'll call you when we're thirty minutes out. You can meet us at the usual place." I remembered the spot by the Executive Terminal where we boarded the Gulfstream on the way to Miami when we were making that Haiti trip. "I'll give my dad and sis a call," I told him. "We'll be there."

Wait a minute, I thought. Billy said, 'we' Who else is on that plane?

I guessed that Mr. Goodman was the 'we' on the plane, but instead, Mal was delighted to see her grandfather and grandmother were on board, their wheelchairs firmly strapped to the floor of the G6. Goodman's executive jet was capable of carrying up to eighteen passengers, but with its configuration, it was nearly loaded with seven. Gloria rode copilot next to Billy, clad as always in a microscopic black dress, sporting perfect, well-tanned legs a mile long and six-inch fuck-me heels. She had to be the sexiest right seat ever to grace a cockpit. I don't know how Billy could keep his mind on the sky. As we rolled down the runway, I pulled up the shade on my window. I don't get to fly much and love looking outside. Moishe cleared his throat to get my attention. "Ah, young Broderick," the old man spoke up. "Mr.

Goodman requests you leave the shades pulled down for the short flight as our destination is, shall we say, rather discrete. We'll only be in the air for an hour or so." He smiled and made that little temple with his fingers, a habit I'd seen Moishe display many times on our trip to Haiti.

Like my dad, I have a good sense of direction. But the Gulfstream banked just after take-off and circled Key West for ten minutes before leveling out and climbing to cruising altitude. So, I had no idea if we were heading north, south, east, west, or straight up to Mars.

Gloria came back from the cockpit after take-off and served beverages. Rum and coke for Dad, and sparkling water for everyone else. (Mal had weaned me from root beer the day she got back.) Mallory had gone to the back of the plane just after takeoff, squatting between Golda and Moishe, and appeared engrossed in conversation. I was left to myself upfront and like my dad, who could sleep while propped up in a phone booth, dropped off into a nap. That dream came again.

This time, I was aware that it was sometime in the middle of the afternoon. We walked from some sort of deck down a flight of stairs and walked along that hall, always with a metal floor. I could hear that sound in the distance, 'Ka-thump, ka-thump!

The dream was cut short by a sharp bump when I was jerked awake as the Grumman G6 touched down. I expected Billy to land as smooth as a bride's kiss with the fragile cargo on board, but the big Grumman rumbled down the rough, uneven runway like a dump truck on a dirt road. As little flying as I have ever experienced, even I could feel him lean hard on the brakes and thrust reversers. This must be a short strip. As we pulled to a stop and turned to park, I sneaked the right side window open a crack. I whistled to myself at the little less than a hundred feet of runway left from where we stopped. Billy whirled the jet, pulled a few yards off the strip alongside two other propeller-driven aircraft, and shut down.

Moishe spoke from the back of the plane, "Ladies and gentlemen, you are welcome to disembark ahead of us and proceed to the wedding venue." Holding his arms wide at the mobile chairs he added, "It will take a little strong-arm effort before the two of us can tag along."

We filed down the airstairs, and I guessed a few things about our location without knowing the exact spot on the map. The warm tropical air, palm trees in the distance, and a sapphire-blue ocean said we were in the tropics. "Saint Somewhere," Dad muttered under his breath in a stage whisper. Looking around, he added "No tower, no hangers, no buildings. This was a strip built solely for drug running back in the day, or," he said with a worried look, "maybe last week." Taking a deep breath of the air, he added with some confidence. "I would guess we're someplace in the Bahamas, or maybe the Turks and Caicos." Dad has been about everywhere on the planet. If anyone would know where we might be, he would. Pointing at the other airplanes on the field, he added, "Beechcraft King-Airs. They must be for the help." We walked down the airstairs to an honest-to-goodness red carpet that stretched across the field toward the beach. At the foot of the stairs were three balloon-tired mobility carts, built for use on the sand. I would guess the third one was for Goodman.

As we followed the carpet over the dune toward the beach, I heard Billy spool up the big jet, I assume to fetch another guest or guests. When we topped the hill, I was amazed at the sight below. On a deserted beach, a little city had sprung up, complete with tents, a big open-air covered dining table with chairs, and a big buffet, complete with shrimp on ice, crawfish, a big cake, and enough champagne, beer, and booze to put Captain Tony's to shame.

"No chairs?" I asked, noting the obvious lack of seating in front of the ceremony location. "Everybody here is either guarding, in mobile chairs, or part of the ceremony." I whirled around at the familiar voice. Coming out of the tent, dressed in white linen slacks and a white guayabera shirt, David warmly welcomed us. "Last time I saw you," I observed, "you were waving bye-bye from the *Never on Saturday* in Acapulco Bay."

"I couldn't miss my sister's wedding," he exclaimed. "Billy dropped me off here two days ago to help set up." Swinging his arms wide, he asked, "Like?"

"Amazing," Dad remarked, and then added, "You look like an extra in the *Streets of Laredo*." That made David laugh, but I didn't have a clue what he meant. Pointing at the tent he just

117

walked out of, he informed, "There's an outfit for you and your dad, just like this one. I took the liberty of guessing sizes. Forgive me if I was wrong."

"Goodman's 'assistant' Gloria told us that shorts would be okay," I answered. I had no intention of dressing like Ricky Ricardo.

"What Mr. Goodman says and what he means are often two different things. His 'suggested' attire should be taken as a mandate. What I'm wearing will be appropriate apparel for the ceremony. I've been tagged as a groomsman."

"I don't need to put on that getup," Dad pointed out.

"Umm, yes, you do," I admitted. "You're my best man."

He looked stunned, "And I wasn't informed of this development before because?"

"So, you wouldn't organize a wild bachelor party with strippers, hookers, two German Shepherds, and a Shetland pony," I answered.

"I'd never do that," Dad said, defensively. "Besides, do you know how hard it is to rent a pony in Key West?" Smiling, he added, "I've tried."

Swarming around all the food was a dozen or so tough-looking dudes, all looking completely out of place in this setting. They all had on three-piece dark suits, and they were all carrying some sort of gun hanging on a sling. Without me asking, Bric pointed out, in his stage whisper, "HK MP5, fully automatic machine guns." He added admiringly, "These boys have got some nice toys."

"Might as well be a Daisy BB rifle, or a bazooka, for all I know," I remarked sarcastically. "A gun is a gun. They all look alike to me."

On the beach was a *Chuppah*, assembled out of local materials, mostly bamboo and stripped palm fronds. Dad whispered a phrase I'd heard a dozen times, "Close your mouth, Brody. You're gonna let flies in." While I was ogling the surroundings, I almost forgot Mallory. She snapped me to my senses, with a peck on the cheek. "Ta-Ta, hubby to be." She said, flushed with excitement. "Your sister and I have a little preparation work to do." She gave her brother one of those ribcage-cracking hugs and picked up her ever-present rollaboard suitcase. Mallory and Mary Beth waved at us, and then marched toward one of the tents, holding hands and giggling like two sisters that had known each other for a lifetime. Still curious, I asked David. "Do you know where we are?"

"Not a clue," he admitted. "I was told to keep the shades down all the way and not to ask questions, I'm sure as you were." Looking at his surroundings, he added, "Definitely not Kansas, or New York. Someplace tropical and remote. Mr. Goodman has friends in low places."

"What about the firepower?" Dad asked, pointing at the rise. "There's enough artillery up there to put down an insurrection." He added with a thought, "Or start one."

"I've known the old man since I was a little boy," David said with a sigh. "In all those years, I have never seen him outside his compound in Manhattan, or the back of his airplane. He was traveling in a DC3 when I was a boy. He's upgraded a bit since. He has friends and he has enemies. He just wants to have ample security while he attends the ceremony."

"Well, that's a lot of security," I remarked. "It's enough guys with guns to make the wedding scene in *The Godfather* look like a kindergarten birthday party."

"Mister Goodman is a peaceful man in a violent world," David answered. I could tell he was choosing his words carefully. "Along the way, he's made a few enemies. That's why this location is so discrete. We don't think anyone will know he's here, but he hasn't lived to be an old man by not covering his bases, so to speak."

Turning around, David announced over his shoulder as he walked away, "Well, I've got some things to do." Pointing at the food, he said with a welcome wave, "Enjoy the buffet and the booze. I'll see you soon."

That left dad and me to wander down to the food. I dove into the shrimp mountain, while Pop picked up the rum and started looking for a mixer.

As they say, to each his own.

As the afternoon wore on, I had put a pretty good dent in those shrimps, and Bric had got outside a fair portion of the rum, without any apparent ill effects. Looking back, I think we both had a little too much of both, but hey, you only get married once. At least one marriage is the limit for me. Hearing a noise to the north, (provided we were in the northern hemisphere, I saw the Gulfstream circle and land again, and Moishe raised his water glass. "That would be our guests of honor, Mr. Goodman and Rabbi Saperstein arriving."

A few minutes later, the third mobility cart trundled over the rise, followed by a man in a grey suit, a big black beard, and a white yarmulke on his balding head. The man in the cart, if possible looked older than the Cohens. It was then I noticed all the suits suddenly were at attention, surrounding our little event and facing away from us with their machine guns unslung. As if on cue Mallory and Mary Beth emerged from their tent, dressed in matching blue, off-the-shoulder dresses. She walked up to me and awarded me with a kiss. The tradition of keeping the bride and groom separated until the ceremony is not a part of Jewish culture. "You have never looked more beautiful," I said in a hushed voice, tears in my eyes.

Then Mallory saw Goodman and ran up to him. *"Sandak!"* she cried. Mallory told me before that she always called him Sandak, Hebrew for Godfather. She gave him a warm gentle embrace and kissed his bald forehead. He didn't offer to shake my hand. "Forgive me," he said, in a croaking voice not much louder than a whisper. "I'm an old man and have grown to fear frequent contact." It didn't stop him, I noticed, from giving Mallory the hug, slipping her a thick envelope in the process.

They talked quietly for a moment, and then she motioned me to come over. He gave me a stern look up and down, and said in a croaking voice, "So you're the young man that defiled my goddaughter." It wasn't a question but a statement. I froze, not knowing how to answer. I saw my life flash before my eyes standing in front of the closest thing to a *real* Godfather I'll ever meet. He must have seen the fear in my eyes, and his voice softened.

"Not to worry, young man. Moishe and Golda have given their blessing, and all present approve of this union today." He smiled and changed the subject to help put me at ease. He added, "I never got the chance to express my gratitude for the clever way you rescued my gold Royals in Haiti. I trust you received your fair share of the commission?" I did get well paid, but I never saw the money. Dad had added it to his investments, safely holed in a long-term, low-risk fund in both our names. "Yessir, thank you very much," I stammered. It was all I could think to answer.

Clapping his hands, Goodman announced. "Shall we commence the event? I would never miss this day, but I must apologize that I'm not accustomed to being outdoors much and wish to spend as little time in the open as necessary." David caught the hint. Holding his arms up he announced, "Ladies and gentlemen, we can begin in a few minutes. Please come forward." He would have normally said please be seated, but everyone that wasn't in the ceremony was seated in power chairs. It wasn't until then I noticed that along with the Rabbi, David, Mr. Cohen, and Mr. Goodman were both wearing yarmulkes now. "Mallory! I forgot my beanie!" Ever prepared, with a twinkle in her eye, she reached into a dress pocket and held up a black skullcap. "You'd lose your head if it wasn't bolted on. I knew you would forget so I packed it for you." David took the cap from Mal and pinned it to the back of my head.

The things we do for love.

The ceremony was a blur. It was formal enough to suit Goodman and the Cohens, and informal enough to suit the location. I really can't remember most parts, Mal and I had met with a rabbi months before so I knew what I was supposed to do when I was supposed to, kiss at the right time, and stomp on a glass at the end.

"I apologize that I will not be able to stay for the reception, or provide my jet for your return," Goodman said. "I have pressing matters in New York this evening after I take Moishe and Golda back to Miami. You will have to settle for one of my King-Airs. My pilot will drop your father and sister off in Key West, and then take you anyplace you choose in the United States, Canada, or Mexico." He pointed at the envelope in Mal's hand. "I've taken the liberty of including a little walk-around money." With a wave and a smile, he gave a mock-stern look. "Be good to this girl. Mallory is the closest thing to a child I'll ever have." We said our good-byes to the grands and I pointed out to David, "No reception? There's enough food to feed an army." David chuckled and waived toward the bodyguards, still standing at attention, guns drawn. "After everyone is in the air, be assured that army, and for that matter, I, won't let any of that food go to waste." Mallory and I gave her brother a big group hug. Bric gave me a firm handshake and with one long, last look at our wedding venue, boarded the King-Air.

After we dropped dad and Mary Beth off at Key West International, the pilot turned toward us from the cockpit. "Bosses orders, kids. Your destination is my command." We looked at each other. Until then, we hadn't even thought about a honeymoon. "I thought that's what we've been on for the last month," I said, laughing. Holding up the envelope, Mallory answered, eyes wide. "It looks like Sandak thought differently. It would be a shame to not honor his wishes and just stay home." We looked at each other, and almost telepathically knew the answer, someplace we have talked about endlessly as a departure someday from palm trees tropical breezes, and islands. Turning back to the pilot, we said in one voice.

"Jackson Hole!"

"We don't have much more packed than a toothbrush, shorts, and a spare pair of flip-flops," I noted. "Hardly clothes for the mountains of Wyoming." Peeking inside the envelope, Mallory held the contents up to me and fanned through the bills. "Those are hundreds," she said, a little amazed. "I think we can do a little shopping when we get there." We headed north, stopped in Denver for fuel, and went on to Jackson Hole Airport, one of the few large airports that's located *inside* of a U.S. national park. The view on approach was almost worth the trip, with incredible snow-capped mountains all around, despite it only being early September. When we landed, the pilot stood in his doorway as we walked out. After shaking hands and giving the bride a hug, he handed her a card. "That's my number," he explained. "Just give me a call a few days before you want to be picked up."

Mallory slid it into a pocket. "That won't be necessary," she told the pilot. "We're just fine to fly commercial on the way home." She added before we went down the airstairs, "Who knows? We might be a few days, a week, a month, or more." She rubbed her stomach, the baby bump hardly showing yet. "But I think sooner than later."

We rented a car, then power-shopped for warm clothes, some camping gear, and hiking boots then on to a market where we shopped like Vikings, with Mallory making wise, low-carb, (and taste-free) dining decisions. Healthy for me, and proper for an expectant mother. After spending a few days enjoying the magnificent sights of Yellowstone, experiencing hot pools, geysers, counting bison, elk, deer, and even a distant grizzly bear, we drove deep into the Tetons. Returning along the Snake River through Jackson Hole, we climbed into the mountains and continued our honeymoon in a tent someplace halfway up the side of some mountain. Skinny dipping in a volcano-fed warm pool, fishing for our breakfast in the morning, and hiking up and down eleven-thousand-foot terrain all day until I thought my heart would pound itself out from the inside for lack of oxygen. Pregnant or not, that girl can *walk*. Give me my Florida Keys where the air is thick enough to chew.

I thought I was in shape until that week.

When we got home to the keys after the honeymoon, we made plans to settle down to married life on the houseboat, diving, and fishing for food. Enjoying a permanent honeymoon, and looking forward to our new family. I can't be a bum for the rest of my life and I started looking for something to get my interest.

It wasn't long after then that something found me.

17

The first thing when we got home from the honeymoon was to check on my dad. Just as we feared, he had reverted to recluse mode, holed up in his place, a shabby rented single-wide on Geiger Key. According to Dad, it was not far from the spot where Karen had been taken to and abused all those years ago. He couldn't stand to stay at Rumpy's old place on Big Pine Key, after both the unpleasant memory of his murder attempt and Rumpy's crossing that rainbow bridge, leaving the house to Rumpy's brother Blotto. He only sneaked out for groceries (and distilled grain spirits) in the middle of the night once a week. We popped in one morning to confront him. "You hide when nobody's chasing you," I counseled him. "The Mexicans have settled down in your apartment in town, and I think they have no interest in leaving the free digs."

"They can stay as long as they want," Dad answered lazily. "I'm enjoying the solitude here more than actually hiding out." He gave a sly smile and remarked. "I spoke to Goodman at the wedding and he told me that the buzz from the groups that wanted me under the lawn has quieted down even farther." He held up a finger, "By the way, he also let me know he has no living family or heirs and is liquidating his assets to prepare for the future." Pointing at Mallory's tummy he concluded. "He's setting up a nice college fund when *that* comes and a healthy trust when it turns twenty-five, as I did for you," he said, pointing at me. "I didn't waste a college fund on Brody. Higher education never seemed to be in his vocabulary."

Mallory looked worried. "Is something wrong with Mr. Goodman?"

"He's in his nineties," Dad answered. "He looks pretty frail, and he won't be around forever. As Kenny Chesney sang, 'Everybody wants to go to heaven, but nobody wanna go now'. Come to think of it," Dad remembered with a chuckle. "From what I gather, heaven probably isn't anymore in Goodman's travel itinerary than college was for Brody."

"It's settled then," I said. "You don't mind being out and about." That was more of a statement than a question. I needed to get my dad out of the house and out of his funk. "Meet us at Hunks on Tuesday, at eight pm." Standing up, I didn't give him a chance to respond. Before he had a chance to form a protest, Mal and I were out of the house and on our way up Geiger Key Road on the way to US1 and back to the Rock.

Tuesday night, Bric walked into the patio of Hunks, surprised by a raucous crowd and a round of applause. Dozens of locals, old friends, male and female, some pretty influential businessmen and women, more than one bar owner, and a couple of bankers joined Mallory and me around the communal hot tub, clapping and cheering. Luis and Jose even came down from the apartment to see what all the commotion was about. I thought my dad was going to take one look, then duck and run. I was proud that he stayed, shaking hands and hugging old friends, many of he had not seen in years.

"What's the big occasion?" he asked, a little confused. I expected his question and was ready with an answer.

I jumped up on a table, called for attention, and announced, "Before we get to the reason for this get-together, I want everyone to look around. If there's anyone here you don't recognize, kick 'em out. Now!" I could see everyone look around, there were a few more hugs, nods, and handshakes. One of the bigwigs from old town spoke up, "All clear, Brody. Tell your father what we're up to."

I banged a pot with a wooden spoon for attention so the crowd would quiet down to a dull roar. "As you know, my father has come back to life after being dead for many years." That got a laugh.

"We thought it was time to get him back out among his friends without being behind a dive mask or a bass guitar." That brought another laugh and a shout. "Or under my wife's dress!" More laughter. I held up my hands for silence. Pointing at my father, I added. "Dad, it's time you do something for this town that you love, and loves you so much, that doesn't make anyone want to string you up in the tree at Captain Tony's." I added with an afterthought, "Yet." At this point, the crowd was roaring. I don't know if it was my humor or the rum drinks that were getting them going, but it made me think for a moment that I might have a career in standup comedy. Then the crowd started a quiet chant that grew into a mutual shout. "Bric, Bric, Bric, Bric!" I banged the pot again to quiet them down.

"Okay," Dad finally said, "what's the big deal?"

I climbed down from the table and held out my arms. "You, Mister Russell Bricklin Wahl, are officially a candidate for Fantasy Fest King!"

I had done my homework. Fantasy Fest kicks off with the Royal Coronation Ball each year, recognizing the men and women who volunteer to run fundraising campaigns in the weeks leading up to the festival. The top fundraisers are crowned the King and Queen of Fantasy Fest, with the runners-up serving as their court. The funds raised benefit AIDS Help, the local organization that has been serving the needs of our HIV and AIDS-afflicted population for more than 30 years.

In twenty-seven years, kings and queens and their courts have raised more than four million. They raised more than $173,000 just a few years ago.

Dad swiped his hands for the noisy crowd to quiet down. He looked like Charlton Heston trying to part the Dead Sea. It wasn't working. "Silence!" He finally bellowed. "The keyword here is 'volunteer', and I ain't. I have no intention of parading down the street one night in my bathrobe on some float in front of twenty-five thousand half-naked drunks, most of them strangers. I might as well paint a big bullseye on my back."

I gave him another big hug and whispered in his ear. "Dad, you told me just a few days ago, that the old man told you the coast was clear, and anyway this is for a good cause." I added one item that I knew might entice him. "And the booze will be free at all the parties, or at least on somebody else's nickel!" He pulled himself away from my hug and backed away, still shaking his head, but I could see he was starting to cave. The 'free booze' line got his attention.

"I'm no king," he said slowly. He perked up a bit with a new thought. "Besides, Fantasy Fest always has a king and queen. I don't have a queen either."

I had him there. Time to pull out my secret weapon. I whistled toward the bar office. "Coming, honey, or at least breathing hard!" Came a voice from the office. Dad's head jerked around at a familiar voice. Out walked a vision that shut the crowd up like an outlaw walking into a saloon in a 'B' western movie. The six-foot, five-inch tall, three hundred pound body was poured into a lime green spandex dress, wearing eight-inch acrylic heels, topped with a flaming red wig and hiding enough foam rubber in the butt and boobs to fill a king-size mattress. Dad was stunned. "Scarlet! I thought you were done with dressing up."

"Bric, honey, you told me a long time ago, 'never say never'. When Brody told me his scheme, I just had to play along." Scarlet wadded through the crowd and gave my dad a big bear hug, nearly suffocating him in the size forty-six 'G' fake boobs. Holding him at arm's length like a rag doll, Scarlett said sweetly. "I'll be your queen any day, dear. Especially for such a good cause." Dad untangled himself from the embrace and backed off out of arms reach. "Uh, remember Kev..ah, Scarlett, my gate doesn't swing that way."

"Don't knock it till you've tried it," Scarlett giggled. "Remember, every name on your contact list's a potential date."

"Alright, Dad," I pointed out. "Your final excuse just showed up, in the flesh, and I do mean flesh," I said, motioning toward Scarlett. "Whadaya say?"

The trees on the patio suddenly became very interesting to my father. He stood there, hands on his hips, looking up for almost a minute, and then finally looked at the crowd, resigned. "Well, I guess it won't hurt, just this once." With that, the crowd cheered and started the Bric! Bric! Bric! chant again. Taking my cap off, I silenced the crowd with a hand. "Alright you gang of pirates, put your money where your yap is."

Scarlet stepped up first, with a wad of money in her hand. "Let me be the first with the most. The gang here at Hunks pooled their tips. Here's a thousand dollars for the pot!" I collected the cash and then held out the cap again while a stream of people lined up with cash in their hands.

As the night wound down, my dad almost looked pleased with the plan. Before he left for home, he gave Mal and me a group hug. "Look on the bright side," he said with a weak grin, "There's no way we can raise enough money to actually win."

Remember what Scarlett said, I thought. *Never say never Bric ol boy.*

After a week of fundraising, it turned out that at least Bric had that part right. Oh, we went to lots of parties, receptions, and events. My father's friends were nice people, (mostly) and the salt of the earth, ranging from homeless bums living under the Garrison Bight bridge to working stiffs, fishermen, musicians, treasure divers, wait staff, Pedicab drivers, and line cooks. Nice people, but more concerned with paying rent, putting food on the table, or having an ample supply of various distilled grain beverages or baggies full of 'herbs' on hand. Donating to a cause, any cause, even as worthy as this one, wasn't high on the priority list. Dollars came in at a trickle, and as we neared the official Fantasy Fest Coronation Ball, it was clear that my dad and Scarlett would be far short of collecting enough money to be selected.

The competition had gone down to the wire, and two other couples were neck and neck. Mallory, Dad, Scarlett, and I went to the coronation, me for the fun and Bric for the booze, knowing we were going to be third in a two-horse race. Dad, looking at the crowd, with many already in costume, mumbled in my ear, "It looks like a cross between an alien invasion and the bar scene in Star Wars."

"Which Star Wars?" I asked.

"Episode Four, which was actually the first one."

"What? I'm confused," I admitted. I had seen all the episodes but didn't remember which went where.

"Forget it," Dad said. "Just watch out for lightsabers."

Whatever, Dad.

We mingled around the Coronation Ball until well into the evening, when the Fantasy Fest organizer climbed up on the stage and banged a pot with a wooden spoon, the proper island mode of attracting attention. As the crowd quieted, she spoke. "Ladies, gentlemen, and uh others," nodding toward Scarlett and a half dozen tastefully attired crossdressers. This year's fundraiser is one of the best in the history of our King and Queen Competition. I want to thank all the candidates for their efforts. As you know it's been a close race up to the wire. We have waited until the last minute to award the winners." She paused for dramatic effect. Holding up a piece of paper in her hand, she continued.

"I had the winners on this piece of paper, but just a few minutes ago, we received a last-minute donation that has changed the outcome. Folks, we just received an anonymous donation," she stopped and spoke quietly to one of the staff. "I just wanted to confirm this. The manager at Wells Fargo just handed me a cashier's check he certifies to be genuine for, would you believe, a half-million dollars! That makes this year, by far, the best fundraiser in our history!" There were tears in her eyes. "Congratulations to our king and queen, and I do mean queen, of this year's Fantasy Fest, none other than our hero, returned from the dead, Bric Wahl and Scarlett!"

Dad had just taken a sip of his rum drink and sprayed it over the first three rows of onlookers. "Wait a minute!" He said, backing toward the door. "Nobody thought I could actually *win* this thing!" Pointing at the runner-up couple, he said as seriously as possible. "I donate my fundraising to Paul and Virginia! There! You're the winner. Have a nice life!" He turned to walk out the door. I caught him by the waist as he passed by me. I could feel him tense as if he was about to perform some commando move and then realized who was holding him. "Come on, Dad," I said as calmly as possible. "It doesn't work that way. You and Scarlett are the winners. Just relax and enjoy it. It's only for another few days."

Scarlett came at him from the other side, putting a hand on his shoulder. Dressed tonight in black Spandex, with stiletto heels and a black wig, she looked as intimidating as Darth Vader in drag and didn't at all appear interested in packing up and going home after all the effort of the past week. "Bric dear, this will be my day, or rather night in the sun, er moon! It's gonna be fun!"

Stabbing my dad in the chest with an acrylic-filled nail, she added. "You said yourself, you owe me your life. Just consider this payback time." She stood back, struck a pose, and put a hand on her hip. "I ain't gonna pass up riding down Duval Street in a ball gown in front of thousands of admiring drunk tourists. This is the biggest target-rich audience in history for me. Don't let me down, boss!"

Scarlett had him there. I can count more times than I have fingers on one hand, starting back as far as my fourteenth birthday when this Amazon crossdresser had helped rescue my father's ass, and Bric knew it. I watched his shoulders sag a little when he knew there was no way out. Nodding his head, he admitted, "Okay, my friend, I'll go along, just for you. But understand, I won't climb on that parade float unless I'm half-popped. That will be a night to tolerate and a weekend to forget." He looked puzzled. "But who the heck came up with that much money? I don't know anyone that would be willing to part with a half-million bucks. I mean, I do know a few people that have that kind of resource, (I thought about two old Jewish men in wheelchairs), but w*hy*?"

The truth would turn out to be stranger than he could imagine.

Dad was disappointed to be missing part of the Goombay Festival, but the organizers insisted he attend a function during the week on Stock Island in the harbor across from the Hogfish Bar and Grill.

"You have to come," they stressed. "This party is being held by Leonardo Lombardi." Mallory, who is always up on current politics, clued me in. "Leonardo is known better as 'Lennie Bucks, the ex-congressman from Illinois. He was rumored to be a crooked politician, and was about to be indicted for bribery, graft, and selling political favors when he got voted out of office." She looked at her phone for more current information, smiled, and looked up. "Now he's a lobbyist for some big mining conglomerate. Nobody can prove it, but he's still thought to be wheeling and dealing on the other side of the law and is reputed to have more than one politician in his pocket. He's so crooked he couldn't lay straight in bed if he tried." Continuing to look at Google, Mal came up with one final tidbit. "Two other items. His girlfriend's sister is married to one of our city commissioners. I'm sure that's what brought him here, and he's known to have a taste for young girls." Mallory frowned, looking at Lennie with disgust, and added. "Genuine one hundred percent slimeball."

We were given the location to Lennie's 'Yacht', and the next Tuesday, we drove the royal couple out to Stock Island. Scarlett, sitting in the back seat of the topless Jeep Wrangler, groused all the way about the wind ruining five hours of hair and makeup. "Don't complain, Scarlet," Dad remarked, "At least you can take that mop off, sit it on the sink and brush it out when we get there!"

Scarlett's answer was priceless, "Just like you can with your teeth, boss!" and gave my dad a punch in the ribs that would have sent a normal person to the E.R.

When we got to our 'destination' we were in front of a tired-looking converted trawler that had definitely seen its better day. Climbing out of the Jeep, dad noted the name on the stern *Bucks Up* and remarked, "That tub is older than time, and I'll bet it's slow enough to paint. I wouldn't be surprised if it doesn't collapse under the weight of that crowd and sink on the spot." I looked on deck and it appeared that the dignitaries were already there, including the losing candidates, commissioners, their wives or significant others, local politicians, and various VIPs. I could see Bric tense. He said with finality, "We're here to say hi, shake some hands, drink their booze, and get the fuck out as fast as we can." He looked around with his arms folded, unimpressed. "This tub couldn't haul garbage for *Seaglass*," he observed. Looking around, he pointed out, "Look at all the rust, the broken hinges half-hanging off the door, and all that dirty furniture. I would be embarrassed to tie up next to this scow. Oh well, we're not here to judge a boat. Let's get this over with."

Dad's reluctance to mingle was starting to wear me out. I felt like I was trying to pump air into a leaky tire. Babysitting my father for a week wasn't my idea of a fun time. Well, at least it would be over soon.

Dad and Scarlett spent the next hour shaking hands and kissing cheeks. I stayed close to him, partly as his casual bodyguard and partly to make sure he didn't bolt for the ramp and run screaming into the dark. Eventually, we were introduced to the host, Lennie Bucks. When I shook his hand, I felt like I needed to wash. My bullshit meter pegged almost immediately, and I could tell from the way my father was standing he wasn't impressed either, but he went through the motions and made casual conversation with a big wig.

"So, Mr. Wahl, I hear you were in the Navy," Lennie said. "Thank you for your service." He said, almost mechanically and obviously without conviction. He looked questioningly, "Viet Nam?"

I could tell Bric was choosing his words carefully, wondering where this was going, and answered. "I could have gone to Southeast Asia as an eighteen-year-old wet-nosed kid, but got a high draft number and waited a few years before joining the Navy."

Lennie tried to look impressed past his boredom. "Midshipman? Annapolis?" He asked.

"Hardly," He laughed. "Just a lowly grunt, seaman first class."

"Don't sell yourself short," Mallory interjected, standing nearby. "You served with the Navy SEALS."

Lennie, gave a low whistle, now visibly impressed. "SEAL, eh. Did you see any action?"

Dad shook his head. "Not really. I was too late for Vietnam and too early for the Middle East." Then he recalled. "Oh, there was that little thing in Grenada. Class A cluster fuck from the word go. We parachuted in, did a little shooting, a lot of hiding, and helped rescue some college kids."

Lennie kept pressing. "Any medals?" he asked

"Oh, we all got a campaign medal. We called it the 'Alive in Eighty-Five' Medal. The conflict was in eighty-three but it took a few years for them to come up with some bling. Just more gingerbread for your dress-whites. I was already out by then." Bric looked a little sheepish. "Uh, I also got a Purple Heart."

Lennie Bucks put his arm around Bric and led him away from the crowd. I followed, just in earshot. "I know people," Lennie said to Dad. "I can get you a distinguished service medal with a few phone calls."

"For being shot in the ass?" Dad said sarcastically. "Look, Lennie, I appreciate the offer, but I don't need any more medals cluttering up a drawer. Not to be disrespectful, sir, but I'm just here to thank you, to do a little glad-handing, drink your rum, and make a fast retreat." He finished by looking at his dive watch. "We have several other commitments tonight." (*We do? News to me.*)

133

Before saying goodbye to Lennie Bucks, he realized it might be appropriate to make a little more small talk with this crook.

"I've got a little sailboat." (*Seaglass* is little? That's news to me.) "My family has been connected with the sea for generations. Do you cruise much?"

"Hardly ever. We mostly use *Bucks Up* to entertain, ah certain people in the middle of Chesapeake Bay." He held his arms out and added. "Ain't she a beauty? *Bucks Up* is a converted 1924 fishing trawler. (Yeah, I thought, and that's when she was last painted.) We get by with a crew of four and a cook." Digging Bric in the ribs with an elbow he added with a sneer. "That doesn't include a dozen or so girls when we're entertaining." I could tell Dad was looking for a way out of this chat. Reaching out to shake his hand as a way to exit, he asked, "So, you staying for the parade on Saturday?" If it was possible, Lennie's smile got bigger and more smarmy. "I wouldn't miss it for the world. Lots of drunk girls looking for a party, lots of booze, and they hardly ever check I.D., if you know what I mean. The younger the talent, the better. I'll fly out next week and let Leonid and the boys take *Bucks Up* home, hopefully after they sober up." He gestured toward a swarthy-looking guy in a blue windbreaker hovering a short distance to his side. I thought to myself, 'more bodyguard than crew' and I figured there was a gun under that windbreaker. With another slimy grin, he added, "She has a completely outfitted soundproof party room belowdecks, perfect for the right kind of party if you get my drift."

I thought Bric was going to throw up right there. I almost expected him to punch this slimebag, especially with the mention of a Russian crew, but instead, he just shook Joe's hands with finality, nodded without another word, turned, and walked away. Grabbing somebody's drink off a server's tray as it passed by, gunned it down in one gulp, set the glass on a rail, and took me by the arm.

"I wasn't going to tell him they check lots of I.D during Fantasy Fest. I hope they throw him in jail for drinking with a minor." Turning to go, he rounded up Scarlet with a glance and said firmly, "Let's blow this popsicle stand. I've kissed enough babies for the night."

"Babies?" I said looking around at the all-adult crowd, I didn't understand.

"Just a figure of speech," was all that he said.

After weeks of campaigning with that surprise ending, days of prep, and hours of staging, the Fantasy Fest parade was almost an anticlimax. I've never been that big on the week, other than always enjoying the Pet Masquerade. Mallory's no prude but isn't interested in sharing unnecessary views of certain body parts with strangers. I have heard that Bric and Karen participated a few times when they were non-people, giving them a chance to mingle unnoticed in public while they wore costumes. I never had proof, but knowing them, I suspect they didn't want to draw attention by overdressing.

Enough said.

Since dad and Scarlet were celebrities, the seats were better at the Pet Masquerade for the royal couple and family. After the pet party, we mostly just hung around Hunks for the week, except for a few royal obligations. It was living proof, that not everybody looked good naked, but who am I to judge. I just sat there all week drinking root beer on the rocks, while Mal sipped her club soda with a twist, pointing and smiling at the partiers on Duval, laughing out loud at some of the people in their dress, or lack of.

Bric found out fast this wasn't just a ride down Duval Street on a Saturday night in a parade float. I likened it to a bunch of baby birds in a nest trying to get that worm from mom. Everyone wanted a photo op with the newly crowned king and queen. Mallory and I made it our mission to make sure the king showed up, sober, well dressed, and properly 'kingly' at all the events during Fantasy Fest week.

After numerous required public appearances every night, we finally got to Saturday and parade day. The instructions were vaguely clear. "Be *here*, about six, sit *there* on the float. Wave to the tourists, get off at the end, and you're free to party all night. Bric was half in the bag from the free rum by five, so I recommended to the committee that the King's seat have seatbelts. When they told me that wasn't possible, I found a length of cotton rope, handed it to Scarlett, and whispered, "tie him on if he starts to fall off." I added, "Switch him to club soda on the rocks with a twist as soon as he doesn't notice. Hopefully, he won't catch on."

We left the staging area near Fort Taylor and headed to the south end of Duval at the finish, so we could pour Bric into the Jeep and get him safely to our houseboat. I was sure he had no business driving up the keys. We pulled up a couple of chairs, sat down, and waited.

And waited.

And waited.

I guess I should have known better. I love this rock but it can't do anything on time, from an airline, a bus route, a cab, or a parade. Scarlett finally texted me at about eight-fifteen to let me know the seven pm start was finally just about nearly almost underway. After turning down Whitehead, right on Front Street, and south on Duval to the end, it was well past ten-thirty before the first float came into sight. We endured the procession for another hour before the last float came into view with the royal 'couple' on board. Before the float stopped at the end of the route, Scarlett jumped, kicking off her nine-inch platform heels as soon as 'she' hit the pavement, and pulling the pink chiffon ball gown over her head in the next instant. Next to go was the artificially padded butt, the bra and falsies, and finally the platinum blonde wig.

"Good-bye Scarlett, hello Kevin," he announced to the world, barefoot now and wearing nothing but a skin-tight black speedo, his body glistening with oil. "I'm glad the night is young and I'm properly dressed for a party," Kevin said. Pointing north, he said with a cheer, "Ta ta! See you soon. I saw a good time developing when we passed the Pink Triangle near Bourbon Street, 801, and La Te Dah. I made at least three dates from the float." With that, he pushed through the crowd and out of sight. That left us looking back up at the float, where Bric was tied to his throne, as requested, sound asleep and snoring loudly. Shaking my head, I climbed up, untied the ropes, and shook him awake, ducking two roundhouse punches while he came to. "Easy there, Cowboy, time to come home," I said gently. I should have known better to wake an ex-SEAL up from a deep sleep. I learned that lesson long ago. Now wide awake, he stood up, stretched, and bounced off the float like a twenty-year-old, more nimble at that time of night than I was. Without the slightest indication of all the rum that must be inside him, he exclaimed, "Well, that was a hoot, but I'm glad it's over. That's gotta be the only event in the world where the participants wear more clothes than the spectators."

I touched his arm and pointed toward the parking lot. "The Jeep's over that way," I said, "We'll give you a ride to the houseboat. I hope you don't mind the couch tonight. We can take you back up to your car in the morning." Nodding toward Mallory and her growing baby bump, I added, "It's late."

Dad stopped and turned to walk back up Duval. "Scarlett wasn't the only one to get a date for tonight. I'll see you in the morning."

The son was about to lecture the father for once when he laughed, "It's not what you think. Luis and Jose were outside of Hunks on the street when we passed by. They invited me up to my place for a nightcap when I was done. It's not too far, and it's a good night for a walk, and the only place I could find parking in crazy town was my own garage. Anyway, *my* couch is a lot more comfortable than *your* couch. And," he finally said looking at the crowd of scantily dressed female tourists surrounding us, both young and old, "The spectating on the way ain't half bad either. Who knows," he added with a smile, "I could get lucky on the way too. Meet me at the apartment tomorrow morning." He waggled a finger at me, "And don't be afraid to sleep in."

Before I had the chance to protest, he turned, and with a Queen Elizabeth-style wave, parted the crowd and disappeared into the night.

If I had known how the next few days would develop, I wouldn't have taken no for an answer.

We honored his wishes the next morning, stopping at Blue Heaven for a yummy egg-white omelet (boring). It was at least fun to feed the baby chicks that were underfoot with half of my unbuttered whole-wheat toast. After breakfast, we drove over to my dad's apartment behind Hunks, parking in the alley behind the bar. I reached into the flowerpot next to the garage entry, where he always keeps the key, both to let guests in and so he doesn't lose it on late nights after committing some sort of indiscretion.

It wasn't there.

137

"What do we do?" Asked Mallory. "Can he hear us knock from down here?"

"Dad always has a backup," I answered. "I bet he hid a second key." Reaching above the doorjamb, I slid my hand across the top and smiled. "Right here." And pulled down the spare key. We unlocked the side door and stepped into an empty garage. "His car is gone. He must have forgotten we were going to come over this morning and already headed up the keys."

"Nice of him to let us know," Mallory groused, sarcastically. I yelled up the stairs, "Good morning!" And noticed the door to the apartment at the top of the stairs was open a crack. "Strange," I said to Mal. "First no key, then no answer, and the apartment door is open. Maybe they all went to breakfast." We walked up the steps, and I knocked on the door jam while I looked into the room. With the blackout shades pulled, the room was dark as night.

"Hello?"

No answer. I reached beside the door and flipped the lights on to a stunning sight. It looked like a tornado had hit the room. Lamps were broken, a chair was tipped over, and there was a shattered drinking glass all over the floor. On the table was some loose rope, pictures had fallen off the wall, and an empty bottle of Rum lay broken on the countertop next to the house key. There was also some blood on the carpet.

And two motionless bodies.

Southernmost Son

Wayne Gales

18

Mallory didn't hesitate, brushing past me. She kneeled over the nearest inert figure and gently touched the carotid artery on his neck with an index finger. She turned toward me, "Dead. He's already cold. He's been here for hours." There was no need to check on the other figure. He was lying on his back, and his neck was at an awkward angle that confirmed his fate without checking. "I think I recognize them," Mallory suggested. "Is this Luis and Jose, your father's house guests?"

I didn't need to inspect the bodies too carefully to identify my friends. Their small size, dark skin, leather sandals, and clothes confirmed her suspicion. "It's them alright." I agreed. Looking around, I asked the obvious. "Dad was supposed to meet them last night. Where is he? Luis and Jose must have been killed trying to protect him." Pulling out my phone, I started to punch 911. "I need to call the cops."

Mallory held up a hand in a stop motion. "Wait. Think for a moment," she said, calmly. "One has a broken neck, and the other one," she pointed to the figure whose neck she had touched. "It looks like he died with a crushed throat. No guns, no knives, just someone that knows how to kill someone quickly and efficiently barehanded." Mallory looked grim and said with a puzzled voice. "There are many people in the world that have that skill," she hesitated for a moment then added, "including me. But I only know of one other person that lives in Key West." She looked at me, her face drained of color.

"Your father killed Luis and Jose."

I stood in the middle of the room, almost sick to my stomach looking at the dead people, even sicker now to think my father had committed murder. Mallory stood up from the body, came over, and gave me a warm hug. "I think I know your father by now," she said, "Bric isn't a violent person unless he's provoked. I think he must have had a good reason for this," she motioned across the trashed room and the bodies with a sweeping arm. "I don't know why, but he must have been in danger to let all this happen. Do you have any reason to suspect Luis and Jose would have a motive? Robbery?"

"I had to search all over to find them in Acapulco. They came with us on *Seaglass* unknown to us, without passports, and planned to sneak into the US." My brow furrowed with concern. "I spent a lot of time with them in the water. You learn a lot about someone when you dive together. None of this makes any sense." Then I had a thought. I went to my dad's nightstand next to the bed and pulled the drawer open. In it was the handwoven wicker basket that looked like a duck with his collection of ancient pieces of eight and several gold doubloons, all worth thousands of dollars, "It certainly wasn't a robbery," I remarked. Rummaging further through the drawer, I found my grandfather's pocket knife, a few other loose silver *cobs* he had collected from various wrecks, and some other nick-nacks, acquired over the years. It was also where he kept his seldom-used cell phone.

And it wasn't there.

My hand shook as I punched his number on my phone. Where was my father? The phone rang three times, and I expected it to go to voice mail when it answered. I didn't hear anyone speak.

"Dad?" I asked. An unfamiliar voice with a bad accent answered. "We've been expecting your call, Brody. Your father is our guest." He spoke quickly, like he thought we were tracing the call, (As if that technology was at our disposal). An unfamiliar banging sound could be heard in the distance. He continued in a dire voice, "Let me warn you, do not call the police. If we learn the police are involved, you will never see your father again."

The phone connection was terrible and hard to understand, between the thug's bad accent and static on the line. My heart was pounding. "You must be far away," I tried to get a hint of where they might be. "What do you want?"

"A million dollars." He answered, almost confident that it was not an unreasonable request. "You have seen the movies. Unmarked bills in mixed currencies. Put them in two suitcases. We will tell you where to deliver. You have one day. No more. I remind you, no police!" He had to raise his voice to get over that pounding noise and repeated twice to be clear with all of that static.

"This call has gone too long. I will call you back later with instructions." He finished with the same threat, "Remember, no authorities may be contacted or your father dies!"

"But," I started. Before I could speak, the phone went dead. What a gut punch.

I sat down on the couch and put my head in my hands. I looked up at Mal and told her, "I don't know how to get my hands on a million dollars. Bric has all of our money tied up in some investment. I don't even know how to access it." I was frustrated. "What do I tell these guys?" I pointed to the dead bodies in the room. "And what do we do about them, if my father is the person that killed them? Do we tell the police?" I put my head in my hand again, fighting back tears.

Thank heavens Mallory was a calming voice. "First things, first," she counseled, then brightened. "Come to think of it, there might be one person that we can discuss both problems with. Let me have your phone." Without looking up, I held it out to her. "What, or who, do you have in mind?" I asked. Mal was already punching up a number. "Mr. Goodman please," she said into the receiver. "Yes, tell him it's Mallory calling. He will take the call." With the phone up to her ear, I heard a weak voice on her receiver. It sounded weak, almost a croak. Mallory brightened. "Sandak! How good to hear your voice. No, Godfather, all is not well." And she related what we found this morning, that Bric was missing, her assumption that the two dead Mexicans could have been Bric's doing, and told him about the ransom call, and a threat if we involved the police. She put the phone on speaker so I could hear the response. Goodman went from a loving godfather to a cold businessman. His voice sounded weak but, if possible, even calmer than Mallory's. "I assume that those two unfortunate gentlemen are the same men that Moishe hired as divers many years ago and David recently." That was a statement, not a question. How did this man always seem to know everything from so far away? He continued, "I suspect that nobody knows they are in America as they are undocumented individuals." I could almost see him sit there and fold his hands while he considered action. "There's an acquaintance of mine that runs a business in New York. He will give these men a respected and honorable service, followed by cremation. They will vanish without a trace." He paused for this to sink in and added, "The less we discuss this, the better for both of us. Tomorrow morning I will send some associates from Miami to Key West to gather any 'evidence' and ensure there is no sign of their having been a struggle. Now, Broderick, that leaves us with your father. I can get you a million dollars in a day or two. That's not a problem, but currently, I'm in Switzerland on my plane. I won't be back in New York until Monday morning, it will take a little longer than twenty-four hours. Two questions to consider, young man. One, how do you know they won't increase the ransom, once you can provide a million dollars, and two, have you heard Bric's voice?" He added with a dire thought to consider.

"Bric may already be dead."

Southernmost Son

Wayne Gales

19

The thought that my father might be gone, left me devastated. I couldn't imagine life without my friend, my buddy, and the person who took so much effort in making me the person I've become. I just felt hollow inside.

Goodman snapped me out of my funk with decisive direction. "First things first," he said, all business. "Leave that room now. Don't touch a single thing. If the police investigate, I don't believe they would be suspicious should they find either of your prints since both of you have been there often, but it's better to be safe. Lock the doors behind you, wipe the knob, and find the bar owner." I could hear some paper rustle over the phone, "I believe his name is Kevin. Give him the key," (How does he know all this?) "Don't tell him what you found, just that my associates will arrive tonight and ask for that key. Based on the experience in Haiti, I fear the concern that your father dispatched these individuals, for whatever reason, may indeed be the correct assumption. These gentlemen sneaked into our country under false pretenses and made an effort to stay undetected. I also believe their disappearance will be overlooked." I could almost see him smile. He went on. "The people that have your father will undoubtedly call you again shortly. Of that I'm sure. Ask, no demand, to hear his voice. In the meantime, I will arrange to get you funds, should you be able to secure a safe release. It's Sunday, and as I said, I'm out of the country on business."

After thanking Mr. Goodman, we hung up, left the flat, locked the house and garage doors behind us, trying not to touch anything, and walked from my dad's apartment through the back of the bar to the front. As expected, Kevin was there, preparing for a busy day. Sunday after Fantasy Fest is always brisk with visitors getting that last drink in before hitting the road, and lots of non-partying locals, eager to get back outdoors after huddling in their houses for several days to avoid the crowds.

Kevin looked up from his prep work cutting oranges and limes and greeted us with a toothy smile. His ripped torso was shirtless to the waist, and I'm sure his Saturday night was both fun and successful. "Good morning, fine people." Not knowing that

Bric had planned to crash at the flat last night. His smile faded when he saw our faces.

"What's the matter?"

I was choked up and couldn't get the words out, so Mallory answered for both of us in two short sentences. "Bric's been abducted. They are asking for a million dollars to let him go."

Kevin reached for his phone and began dialing numbers. "I've still got friends at the Key West Police Department from when I worked undercover." Before the call went through, I reached toward Kevin's hand and pushed the 'off' button on the phone. "They said no police or they would kill him. I've arranged for the money, and it will be here tomorrow morning. We need to do what they say, at least for now." I fought back tears when I stressed, "We better do what they ask."

Kevin abandoned his prep work, brought us both coffee and juice and then joined us at the table. "What happens now?" he asked. "We wait for another call," Mallory answered. Pulling a pad and paper out of her bag, she started making notes. "Let's write down what we know. One, there are two dead bodies in Bric's flat."

"What?" Kevin said, looking toward the back of Hunks in fear. "Dead bodies? Who?""Mal, we were told not to let anyone else know." I looked at Mallory with concern. "But I agree with you that Kevin needs to know. After all," I said nodding toward our friend. "You are family. We don't dare notify the police, at least not yet." I looked back at the flat. "We think my father may have either killed Luis and Jose or at least had a part in their deaths." I dug in my pocket and handed Kevin the apartment key. "Some people will come here later and ask for this key. I suggest that you don't ask questions and stay away from my dad's apartment." Kevin took the key with shaking hands. "What do we do now?"

"Wait for a call, that's all we can do," I answered. Mallory tapped her pen on a water glass. "We need to get back to what we know," she said with authority. "Brody, is there anything to note about the call?"

I thought for a moment, head in hand, and tried to recall every detail. Looking up, I answered. "Well, the voice was foreign, for one. Mal, any idea what the accent was?"

Writing on her tablet, she made notes. "Definitely Eastern European. Turkish, one of the Baltics, Ukraine, maybe Russian. What else?"

"I could hear some sort of pounding like they were in a factory, and the connection was poor and full of static like they were far away maybe another country."

Mallory kept making notes. Looking at me, she asked, "Anything else?" I wracked my brain, trying to remember any other details. Exasperated, I confessed, "Nothing else. We just have to wait for another call." I pulled my phone back out. "Should we call them?" I asked, looking at Kevin and Mal. "No, not now," Mallory answered. "They said they would call back. When they do, ask for proof he's still alive."

The thought that they might have killed my father sent my head spinning again. "I feel so helpless," I said my head in my hands again. Looking up, I said to nobody in particular, "When will they call?" A familiar voice behind me almost made me jump out of my skin.

"Oh, they will call, for sure." I whirled around and stood.

"Karen, what are you doing here?" Karen Murphy, Bric's old girlfriend sat down at the table. My father had enjoyed, (or endured) a love-hate relationship with her for like, forever. He met her in Granada during the little uprising there in the eighties, found and lost gold with her, and took many long trips, both by motorhome and boat. They narrowly escaped death on several occasions, and he's proposed to Karen more times than I need to know. She walked out on him for the last, (and what I thought was the final time), about a year ago. "I just came back to the Rock to visit my old haunts, play at Fantasy Fest safely under disguise, and do a little slumming." Her answer was cryptic. After

149

congratulating Mallory and me on our recent nuptials, she got serious.

"Some Guido called me on Bric's phone and left a message. I saw the name on my caller ID, so I didn't answer thinking it was just another midnight drunk call from your dad." Holding up her phone, she continued. "Bric never leaves a message when I don't take his calls so I was surprised to see a voicemail show." She started to tear up. "He said that he had Bric, that he was safe and healthy, for the moment, and wanted a million dollars."

Taking Karen's hand in mine, I tried to comfort her. "We have some friends that can get their hands on the money," I explained. "But Karen, didn't my dad give you half the money he got for all that gold?"

Her answer was almost defiant. "That blood money was bad luck from day one. I've been giving it away to charities as fast as I could." She started counting on her fingers. "Helping the homeless, pet shelters, unwed mothers, and other organizations. I didn't want a dime. Not that helping Bric wouldn't be first on my list, but I just gave my last half-million dollars to a local cause." She clapped her hand over her mouth, realizing what she had just said.

Now, I know how Bric became the King.

Karen was sobbing while she explained. "Bric's a scoundrel, womanizer, a hopeless drunk, and the biggest asshole I've ever met, but he's the only person I've ever really loved. When a friend told me that he was a Fantasy Fest King candidate, I could think of no better organization to give the money to, so I made an anonymous donation in Bric's name." Dabbing at tears she added. "Maybe it was a gesture on my part to admit to myself that maybe the dysfunction in our relationship was as much *my* doing as it was *his.*

Before anybody could say another word, I jumped again when my phone chirped. Seeing Dad's name on the display, I answered and pushed the speaker button so we could all hear. The call was short and to the point, to keep anyone on the other end from initiating a trace.

"Two large hard-side suitcases. One million dollars in all denominations. You have three hours. I will call back."

"Wait," I said as forcefully as possible. "We can get the money, but it will take until tomorrow."

"Then you will never see your father again," came the reply. I could almost see him sneer. He hung up before I could say another word.

"What do we do?" I asked. "Goodman said tomorrow morning. Getting that much cash on a Sunday is hard to do. This dickhead has to know that."

"I've been trained to deal with people like this," Mallory interjected. "He's just trying to scare you. He knows if your father is dead, they won't get a dime." Mal put a hand on my shoulder. "Brody, I know that it's your father, but would it be ok if I spoke to the kidnapper the next time he calls?"

"Be my guest," I answered with a shrug. "I'm not getting anywhere."

We waited another hour before the phone rang again. I punched the speaker button. The same voice spoke. "Do you have the money ready?"

I almost didn't recognize Mallory's voice. She answered with a deeper voice forcibly and controlling, "Whoever you are," she started. "How can you expect us to give you a dime in exchange for nothing? You have given us no proof that Mr. Wahl is with you, or if he's even alive."

The answer made my skin crawl. "Perhaps, we should have a finger delivered to you. That should be proof enough."

Karen mumbled under her breath, thinking the person on the other end couldn't hear. "Maybe they should send his dick instead. Something more recognizable to me and probably half of Key West."

"That could be arranged, Miss Murphy. That is Miss Murphy, isn't it?" Karen's eyes got big and I could see her gulp as she realized the voice had overheard her not-too-quiet comment.

Mallory held a hand up for Karen and everyone else to be quiet. "A finger or any other body part could come from anyone or for that matter, it could be from a dead person," Mal leaned closer to the phone for emphasis. "We need to speak to Bric before any money changes hands." She finished with a forceful, "Now!"

The phone went dead with a click.

151

Mallory had her pad out again, pen in hand. "Think about the call," she said. "Before we forget anything, did we learn anything new?"

I thought for a second. "Same crappy connection with intermittent static, but I didn't hear that banging noise. The factory must work half-days on Sunday." I felt frustrated, "Nothing else." Looking at Karen and Kevin, I raised my eyebrows. "Anything else to add?" Both sadly shook their heads no.

This time it was only fifteen minutes before my phone chirped. I pressed the speaker button again. "Hello?"

A weak, but recognizable voice on the other end only uttered one word.

"Brody?"

I jumped up from the chair and got as close to the phone as possible. "Dad!"

"Are you satisfied?" It was Dickhead's voice. Since he didn't give us a name, I gave him one of my father's favorite labels that he always gives to slimeballs. He gave in an inch with his demands. "You have until noon tomorrow to get the money. I will not wait one minute longer. I will call you in the morning with further instructions." I could tell he was about to close the call, but I came up with another question to keep him on the line for a few moments more. Mal, Karen, and Kevin were listening intently for any clues.

"One last question," I said. "Were Luis and Jose working for you all along?"

"The *inostranets*?" He almost spat out the words, and answered with a quiet chuckle, "Never hire *nekulturnyy* to do the work of a professional." And the phone went dead.

"At least we know Dad's alive," I said with some relief.

"Holding people for ransom is far too common in the Middle East," Mallory pointed out. "My experience says they have no intention of keeping him alive after they collect the money, and I fear contacting the police or FBI won't help with the outcome."

I thought of my dad's wartime buddy for help, but Tim moved to Mexico and is out of the service. Any CIA contact numbers he might have been left with are stored in the phone that's in unfriendly hands.

My wife pulled out her pad and pen again. "Okay, what did we just learn from the call?"

"This time there weren't any static or pounding sounds," I noted. Frowning, I added, "I didn't recognize some of the words he was using."

"I did," answered Mal. "I'm fluent in five languages. Inostranets and nekulturnyy are Russian. *Inostranets* means foreigner in Russian and *nekulturnyy* tags someone that's uncultured or white trash. I don't know how much that info helps, but we now know who has Bric." I could tell she was puzzled by this information. "We just don't know what Russians we are dealing with." She counted on her fingers again. "Are they government agents, the Russian Mafia, or just some freelance thugs?" She looked frustrated. "Knowing who we are dealing with will affect how we should respond."

Kevin stood up. "I guess there's nothing to do until tomorrow." Looking around Hunks, he said with a tear, "I don't even know if I should even open today. All I can think of is my best friend in pain and danger."

"Open, Kevin, and keep busy," I answered, standing up and giving my friend a hug. "Like you said, nothing can be done until they call tomorrow. No sense taking a paycheck away from the staff." Taking Mallory's hand, I added, "We have to make sure the money will be here tomorrow." Pointing at Kevin's pocket, I reminded him. "Don't forget, people will be by later for that apartment key."

"What key?" Karen asked.

"Never mind," Mallory answered for me. "Just some housecleaning people."

I realized that we had left Karen just standing there. "Would you like to meet us here tomorrow morning?" Karen looked torn, then made a decision. "I was supposed to fly home today. I'll cancel my reservation and stay here at least until Bric comes home, or…" She began to cry again. Mallory stepped forward and put her arms around her. "We'll get him home, don't worry." Karen pulled away, dabbing at tears. "I didn't know I still loved him so much," she said, her face in anguish. "If, I mean when he's freed, I think it's time to say 'yes', this time to the question he's asked me so many times before. He may be a scoundrel, but I do care for him."

There was nothing left to do but go home, sit at the table, stare at the phone, and wait. For once in my life, I didn't have an appetite. Mallory knew better than to try to make chit-chat. We did talk to Goodman a few times, confirming that he was on his way home from Europe, that the 'housekeeping crew' was en route, and their duty would be taken care of by morning.

I couldn't even think of sleeping, with everything on my mind, so I just sat at our table with my head in my hands, frustrated and helpless. After what seemed an eternity, Mallory put a hand on my shoulder. "Brody, it's almost two. You need some rest." Pulling me to my feet, she led me into the bedroom. "There's no way I can sleep," I said. "Then just lie down for a while," she urged. "It's doing nobody any good sitting at the table staring at your phone." I knew she wouldn't take no for an answer, so I lay down on the bed, still dressed, and pretended to sleep.

Then came that dream again.

Have you ever been dreaming, and know you are dreaming? It was the first time ever for me and it was weird and bizarre. The dream started like always, but this time there weren't any loud voices. There was still a figure with me, a friend, but I could never tell who it was. There was that noise again, 'ka-thunk, ka-thunk,' faint and distant. As we walked down the hall, I knew from the other dreams to ignore the first few doors on the right and left and go straight to the fifth door on the right. I took hold of the door handle, and unlike the other dreams, it didn't open this time.

Then I heard a voice behind us that I couldn't understand, but I knew it was a threat. We turned and someone was pointing a big gun at my chest. Then I heard a voice.

"Brody! Brody!" I woke up, again in a cold sweat, Mal was shaking my shoulder, "Brody! He's on the phone!"

I sat up, hoping this was all a dream when yesterday's terror came back. Looking at Mallory, I asked, hopefully. "Who's on the phone? Dad?"

Mal's eyes told me 'no' before she answered. "It's the Russian," she said, as calmly as possible. "He wants to know if we have the money."

I got out of bed, groggy, and still dressed from last night. "What time is it?"

She looked at her dive watch. "It's almost nine." Handing me my cell, she urged, "Here, he wants to talk to you."

I didn't bother with greetings and just gave him the answer I knew he wanted. "I was told last night the money will be here later this morning. Once my dad has been freed, I'll tell you where it is."

I almost knew what his answer would be. I could hear that banging noise again. The connection, like before, was terrible. "No, young man, you have it backward. When I have the money in my possession, your father will be released. No sooner. You have three hours."

And the phone went dead again.

In an instant, Mallory was dialing a familiar number. "Sandak," was all she said in a quiet voice. Putting the phone on speaker again, we heard him answer. Like Mallory, he dispensed with any greeting. "I'm back in New York. The bank opens at ten, and Billy will be in the air no later than ten-thirty. You should have the money no later than noon. Billy will call you with an ETA." I tried to thank him, but he closed the call with reassurance and a warning. "Broderick, the money means nothing to me. Your father's safe return is all that's important, but," he paused, "I have a little experience in these matters. As I told you, I have my concerns that, even if the abductors get their money, they will not free your father, especially if he can recognize his captors. Please be careful."

I tried to call the Russian with an update, but he didn't answer. The connection was lousy anyway so I tried a text. *The money is coming from out of state. It will be here not long after noon. How do I get the money to you?* I tried to get a little more info, where are you and where is my father? Are you in the US? After a minute the text answer came back. *We are not far. Tell me when you have the money.*

"Get a shower, so we can go to breakfast." Mal pointed out, "You haven't eaten since yesterday morning."

"I don't have an appetite. Let's just go to Hunks and wait for Billy to call. We'll be a little closer to the airport from there."

155

"Not really," Mallory pointed out, "but we need to stay off the phone and get Kevin up to speed."

We parked and took our usual family table in a corner of the bar. After a week of wall-to-wall naked people, Key West was a ghost town on the Monday after Fantasy Fest. Kevin saw us, brought a tray of coffee, and sat down at the table. Karen showed up a few minutes later, no makeup, hair unkempt. She was a hot mess.

"Ahem," I started, choosing my words carefully, "You look like you've been up all night," I remarked.

"How can anyone sleep when your father is being held, or…"

I tried to put that thought out of my head.

"Any news?" Kevin asked.

"We know the ransom money's on the way, but not much else," I answered. "Did the people come by for the key?"

"About midnight and they never brought it back," Kevin answered, shaking his head. Looking at the back of the bar toward the apartment, I wondered out loud, "Should we go check? I put the spare key back over the door sill."

"Mr. Goodman said to stay away," Mallory pointed out. She pulled her pad and pen back out. Looking at Kevin and me, she asked, "Have we learned anything new?"

"Well, he said he was close," I noted. "That's strange with all that background noise and bad connection." Mallory made notes and added, just realizing, "Bric's car is missing, I hardly think he killed two people, got in his car, and surrendered to the kidnappers." She added with conviction, "They have his car."

I stood up and pulled the Jeep keys out of my pocket. "Let's cruise around town! There can't be that many rust-bucket Toyotas on this rock." Mallory put her hand on mine. "The car could be anywhere between here and Big Pine. That's a lot of roads. Besides," she reminded me, "Remember, he wants the money in suitcases. We need to find at least two, depending on how many small bills Sandak is sending."

I nodded toward Karen as we left. "We'll call you if anything changes." Looking her over I added, as tactfully as possible. "You might want to go back to the hotel and, er, take a shower or something."

I couldn't see any benefit in having her tag along.

We power-shopped Target, loading three cheap hard-side suitcases in the Jeep in just a few minutes. "Let's go to the airport. I want to be there when Billy lands."

Mallory looked at her watch again. "It will be at least an hour and a half before he can get here." Stabbing me in the chest with a finger, she announced. "You, my husband, need food. You're running on adrenalin. I don't want you tapping out at the wrong time," she said with authority. "And," she reminded me, patting her growing bump. "I need to feed this baby. We're going to lunch."

Food was the last thing on my mind, but she was right. She needed nutrition, and besides, there would be no luck arguing. I knew when I was beaten.

"OK my wife, I give. Where to?" She put a finger to her chin for a moment and decided.

"Hogfish."

The Hogfish Bar and Grill is the best bar nobody can find in Key West. Technically, it isn't in Key West, but on Stock Island, and sits on an obscure dead-end street past some of the shoddiest trailerhoods in the Keys. I've been going there since I was riding my Big Wheel and knew the turns. The lunch crowd hadn't arrived yet, which meant our parking spot wouldn't be a ten-minute walk to the bar, always jammed day and night with tourists and locals. We took a table outside by the water, our favorite family spot. I was a local and frequent customer, and the server didn't even ask what I wanted. "The usual, Brody?" She didn't even write it on her pad. "A hogfish sandwich and a root beer?" I nodded absently. I had too much on my mind to think. She turned to Mallory. "And you?" Mal put down the menu and answered, "I'll have the same, except we'll have water instead of soda." She almost had to yell over the construction noise on the other side of the harbor. They were rebuilding the pier, driving new pilings into the bay bottom, and welding cross pieces to them. I could see a big pile of wood on the shore that would be used for the new deck. Suddenly I remembered where I had heard that sound before. Actually, two places. One of them in a dream. Without taking my eyes off the construction, I pulled the phone out of my pocket.

"Mal," I said, slowly, "Do me a favor and walk down to the end of the dock and call me? I want to test something."

She looked at me like I was an alien, but didn't question me, got up from the table, and walked a hundred feet west from the bar. I heard my phone chirp and I answered.

"What's this all about?" she asked. "Just listen," I answered. "Speak up, I can hardly hear you," she responded over the static. "Turn around and look," I instructed. "That static on the phone happens every time that arc welder is on, And," I added. "Does that pounding sound familiar?" I nodded to my right. "I know where they are keeping my dad." She looked at where I was pointing.

Wayne Gales

20

Her mouth flew open as she recognized the boat. Berthed in the same place we last saw it a week ago when we were at the cocktail party. And a few dozen yards away, backed into a parking spot so the license plate was out of view, a familiar rusty Toyota sedan with a dirty tarp covering the back half.

Bucks Up.

I jumped up, ignoring my favorite hogfish sandwich that the server had just put on the table while I was pointing out where I was sure my father was being held. Mallory walked back to me. I pulled my keys out again, then thought better of it. I reached for her hand. "We can walk over there! Come on!"

"Hold on there, Brody," she answered as calmly as possible. "How do you know he's on *Bucks Up*?"

I didn't want to admit that most of what I was going on came from a dream, so I answered with what we both knew. "Remember the night we were on Lennie's P O S boat at the cocktail party? You were standing with me when Lennie Bucks pointed out one of his crew, a bad-looking character, with a Russian name. I was sure he had a gun under his jacket. Slimeballs hire slimeballs and anyway, I wouldn't be surprised that Lennie's in on this. Telling us he's going out of town Sunday morning gives him the perfect alibi. And," I pointed out, "That's definitely Dad's car. It might blend into every other beater car in Key West, but I'm positive that's it."

"What you are saying makes some sense," Mallory answered after a few moments, "and that's all the more reason to not barge into a boat with at least four people, that wouldn't hesitate to kill you, me, or your father. For that matter, Bric knows what at least one of them looks like. There's no doubt they don't plan to ever let him go."

"Then what do we do?" I answered in anguish.

I almost dropped the phone when it chirped in my hands a moment later. It wasn't my dad's number. I hesitated for a moment, then answered. A familiar voice was on the other end. "Hi Brody, it's Billy in the G6 on the satphone. I'll be landing in about fifteen minutes. Do you remember where to meet me?"

161

"I sure do," I answered with a smile. "See you at the Executive Terminal."

I dropped a twenty on the table, leaving the untouched sandwiches, and we left for the airport in the Jeep. We watched the big Grumman jet land and taxi to the pad on the private aircraft end of the field. After a few handshakes and hugs, Billy pointed to the back of the plane. "As requested, a million dollars in mixed non-sequential currency. They are packed in two army duffel bags. That's all I could find with such short notice. I hope that's okay."

"That will be fine," Mallory answered. "We got some other packaging at the kidnapper's request." At the word kidnappers, Mallory began to softly cry. Billy put an arm around her shoulders, and said as confidently as possible, "Mr. Goodman stressed not to worry about the money, just get Bric back." Billy looked at me and added with a frown, "he's concerned about your father's safety, even after the money is delivered." He motioned at the duffel bags and explained.

"I just flew in from Europe to New York on Sunday and I was up before dawn getting the plane ready to come here," Billy noted. "I'm going to spend the night in Key West anyway and get some rest. Is there anything I can help you with?" With a sly smile, he added, "Occasionally I do more for my boss than punch holes in the clouds with this jet."

Mallory pulled her phone out before answering. "We need to call my godfather and fill him in on some developments. He may have some suggestions on how you can help."

She set the phone on a table in the G6 and put it on speaker. "Good morning, my child," came the weak voice on the other end. "Has Billy arrived?"

"Yes Sandak, he's here with us." Mal went on to explain, "And we think we know where Bric is being held." She went on to explain the sounds, the static, and the car. *Bucks Up* was the only probable place near there that he could be, plus the Russian name of Lennie's crew member.

"Ah, our old friend Leonardo," Goodman gave a little chuckle. "I have had dealings with him and his associates a few times in the past. My friends and I try to steer away from his dealings. He gives a bad name to our legitimate practices." After a pause, he continued. "Your deductions sound valid. I have an idea. Would you care to hear my suggestions?"

"Of course!" I almost shouted into the phone. Mallory motioned me to calm down.

"Crooks, being crooks, are selfish, greedy, and suspicious. They won't trust one person to get the ransom money, in fear he would run off without sharing, so at least two, three, maybe all of them will go for the cash, leaving your father unattended, tied up, locked up, or sadly, worse." He paused to let that sink in. "Do you have a place to leave the ransom where it's secure? I'm sure just walking up to the boat with a million dollars and saying, 'Hi, here's the money, can I have my father back?' won't play very well." I thought for a minute and then had an idea. "Mr. Goodman, since they have my father's car, they have his garage opener. They can pull the car into the garage and take the money while I go on *Bucks Up* and get Dad."

"Not 'I'," Mallory interjected, "We."

I tried to look stern, "It's too dangerous Mallory, especially in your condition. You go with Billy and show him where the garage is. You know where I left the spare key. Wait at Hunks until you hear them open the garage door, then call and let me know."

Mallory stood up, her fists clenched, as angry and determined as I have ever seen. Tears started welling up in her eyes. "He's my father too, now," she said through clenched teeth. "Where you go, I go." Pointing toward our pilot, she directed, me like I didn't have a choice. "Billy can drop us back off by Hogfish. Tell him how to get to the apartment, and where the key is. He can go into the garage, put the money in the suitcases, and let us know. He can stay out of sight until the goons show up and text us when they arrive. Then we can go on *Bucks Up* and get your dad. Anyway," she said with a little smile, "I can still outfight you if it comes to that unless they need some boards kicked."

Now I know who that other person was in my dream.

As much as I hated it, her plan was better than mine. Anyway, as Goodman said, they don't trust each other enough to split up. Dad will probably be left alone.

Or...

We forgot that Mr. Goodman was still on the phone until he spoke. "What I hear makes perfect sense or at least the best chance you have of rescuing your father alive. Billy is the perfect person to handle the cash, and Broderick," he added with a quiet chuckle. "Even in her condition, Mallory is a more than capable sidekick."

I knew when I was licked. Billy and I each picked up one of the duffel bags, and walked through the exit gate, pausing long enough to let one of the Key West Police drug-sniffing dogs make a pass by each bag. I had a moment of apprehension since half the large bills in South Florida have at least a hint of cocaine and marijuana, but the dog signaled his approval by turning away from us instead of sitting down, telling his master they contained drugs. We went to the Jeep and I tossed Billy the keys, had him drop us off at the Hogfish, let him know where Dad's apartment was, and gave him instructions on where to find the spare door key to the garage. On the way back to the Hogfish, my phone chirped. "Perfect timing," I said, seeing Dad's name pop up on the screen. I didn't bother with a greeting again and just cut to the details.

"We just picked up the money. We will leave the suitcases in the garage at my father's apartment. I'm sure you know where that is." I didn't want them to know we saw my dad's car next to the boat, so I added for effect, "I think you took his car since it's not in the garage. On the visor is the garage opener. Open the garage, pull inside, close it, count the money if you want, then let my father go. Mallory and I are waiting in our houseboat," I lied. "If you don't let my father go, you will never leave Key West alive."

I could tell he took the phone away from his mouth while they quietly discussed my offer in Russian whispers. Mallory put the receiver to her ear to see if she could pick out any of the conversations. After a sound of laughter on the other end, the voice came back on. He sounded uncomfortable. "We're not sure we want to go back to that place." I had an answer for that.

"Where else can you go to count the money? In the middle of Duval Street? The bar top at Sloppy Joe's? Maybe on the patio at Hog's Breath? Listen, that's the safest place possible. You don't even need to go upstairs, just check the money, load it up, and leave." More muffled sounds, then "How soon will the money be there?" I looked at my dive watch. "Let's say thirty minutes. That would be twelve-thirty. When will you release my father?"

"When we see the cash, I will release him. He will be with us in the car."

That was a development I didn't expect. I thought of a way to respond. "So, you will just let him walk away?"

"That is correct. He will be free and we will leave. Don't try to find us. You will never find us. Remember," he growled, "No police!" And he hung up.

'Bet me', I thought.

I looked at Billy and Mallory with concern. "If they do take Dad along, that complicates things. What do we do?"

Billy sounded confident. "I'll put the money in the garage, and stay nearby. And," he said with that sly smile again, "My bosses 'clean up' crew that came here from Miami Sunday night are still in town. If your father's with them, I'm sure we can 'convince' them to release him." He added with a soft chuckle, "To quote a familiar line in a certain movie, we'll make them an offer they can't refuse."

Mallory spoke up, "I understood quite a bit of that call. One asked if they should take Bric with them, another said yes, put him in the trunk, and the voice on the calls," Mallory nodded toward me. "The one you call Dickhead, said no. Leave him tied up on the boat, and they would see how good he could swim in the ocean when they left – with the spare anchor tied to his feet. That's what caused the laughter."

I shivered with the news but felt a little relieved, "That confirms my dad is on *Bucks Up*. It should be a breeze," I counted on my fingers, ignoring for a moment what Mallory had just interpreted. "They all drive away, we walk on the boat, find Dad, and get the hell out before they get back."

"And when they call, what do you say?"

I hadn't got that far. "I guess ask them where my father is, even if we're safe and far away. I'm positive with a million bucks, they will just come back to the boat and leave as soon as possible. It won't be until then that they learn that Bric isn't there." I gritted my teeth. "I'm not happy that they can just sail off into the sunset with Mr. Goodman's money, but we have to honor your godfather's request that we not involve any authorities."

Before leaving, Billy pointed out. "Remember what I told you. Mr. Goodman said not to worry about the cash, just make sure your father is safe," Billy looked serious. "I know Mr. Goodman. He will address the regrettable deeds these gentlemen have committed in his own way." We watched the Jeep with Billy and the cash drive out of sight. We sat down at the same table we had so hastily departed an hour earlier. The same server walked up, tossed some menus in front of us, and asked, "Do you plan to eat this time, or just order, throw some money on the table, and leave again?" I knew we couldn't just sit here without ordering something so I asked for a couple of diet cokes.

It was almost a half-hour later, across the harbor, that we saw four men pile into Dad's Toyota and drive off. "I hope they don't get to the apartment before Billy has transferred the money into the suitcases," Mal noted. "I'll bet they have guns."

"I gather." I noted, "that Billy can take care of himself. Not to worry."

As the crooks drove out of sight, I stood up, ignoring the untouched drinks that had been set before us, threw a few bucks on the table, and took Mallory's hand. "Showtime," I said. "Let's go get my father. Hopefully, there were only four of them and they left him alone." As we walked away from the Hogfish to go around the end of the harbor, the server called after us. "Next time I'll just rent you that table so you don't waste so much food and drink!" I put a hand up in a feeble wave with my shoulders hunched in case she threw the glasses at us. We approached *Buck's Up* carefully, looking up to see if anyone was still on the boat.

"I don't think they left a guard behind," I said. "At least no one's in sight. Here goes." We got to the base of the ramp, took a deep breath, and walked aboard.

"So far, so good," Mallory said in a whisper. Turning to me, she said. "It's a big boat, where do we start?" She checked the time. "We probably don't have more than twenty minutes before they come back."

"Follow me," I answered, not admitting to my dreams again. "I have a hunch." We found two sets of stairs in the lounge that led belowdecks. The first stairs went directly into the engine room. "Not here," I instructed. "Let's try the other stairs."

"How do you know?" Mal asked. "Shouldn't we check around?"

"I just know," I answered. I didn't have time to explain.

The other set of stairs looked more promising. They led to a hallway with doors on both sides. The deck was bare metal. We walked softly in case we weren't alone. Ignoring the first doors. We went directly to the end of the hallway while I counted the metal doors, one, two, three, four. The last door on the right was the fifth door, with a 'private' sign above it. I tried the handle, instinctively knowing it would be locked. This door was wood and opened inward, not outward like the others. I didn't care anymore that I might make a little noise. "No time to hesitate," I said almost to myself. Without waiting to tell Mallory, I just took a step back and gave it a mighty stomp. The door literally exploded into kindling, leaving a narrow piece of the door swinging on the hinges. We stepped over the pieces into the dark room. As my eyes got accustomed to the low light, I could start picking out features. The wall was covered in whips, chains handcuffs, a bed, a cage big enough for a human, and several other items for which purpose I could only imagine, but I had a good guess. We had found Lennie's private dungeon, the one he bragged to my dad about.

As my eyes adjusted better to the one naked light bulb in the middle of the room, I saw a single chair sitting by itself. Someone was tied to the chair, shirtless, shoeless, slumped over, still and motionless.

"Dad!" We ran to the middle of the room. The figure slowly picked his head up. His face was bruised, dried blood caked his head and shoulders, and one eye was swollen nearly shut. "Brody?" Bric tried to look alert but he was a mess. His voice was not much more than a whisper. "Sorry, it's so cozy down here. I must have dozed off." With a crooked smile over a split lip, he added. "It's about time you showed up. I was getting tired of working these guys over. I almost had them where I wanted. I'm pretty sure one of them broke a knuckle on my thick head."

"Dad!" That was all I could say again. Mal and I hugged him, then looked around for something to cut the ropes with. The knots looked impossible to untie.

"There." Mallory pointed to a table, covered with all kinds of dildos, whips, and sex toys. In a butcher block was a carving knife, every bit of twelve inches long. I shuddered to think what that pig might have used it for. We cut the ropes off and took Bric by the arm. "Can you walk? We need to get out of this tub. They will be back soon."

"I can move if I have to crawl out of here on my butt cheeks and elbows." Looking around the room he added grimly, "The stuff in this room might be for some people's fun, but I can tell you from personal experience, it's multi-purpose equipment."

Dad wobbled to his feet and shook his hands, trying to get the feeling back. After a few minutes, while Mallory massaged his legs to get the circulation back, we put a shoulder under each arm and led him toward the door. As we walked down the hall toward the stairs, we heard a voice coming down.

"I checked out of the La Concha and took a cab. I figured you guys would be busy this morning. Get the money?" He looked up from the stairs, recognized who we were, and started reaching inside his jacket.

Lennie Bucks

One of the first things Mallory taught me was "If you're gonna fight, fight dirty, and don't warn. Her training took over. Without a wind-up, I let go of my dad, stepped forward, and kicked Lennie so hard in the crotch that I thought his balls were going to pop out of his ears. Mal took it from there. Still holding up Bric with one arm, she reached toward Lennie's bent-over figure with her right hand and shoved his head so hard into the wall, I swear I heard a crack. The figure slumped to the floor, motionless.

"Did you kill him?" I asked.

"I hope so," spat Mallory, still holding my father up. "If I didn't kill him, after what you did, I'll wager he'll have to adopt if he ever wants kids."

I got back under my dad's arm. Mallory stooped down, and slipped her hand inside his jacket, pulling out a small black pistol. She pulled the slide back a little to confirm there was a live round in the chamber, smiled, and slipped it into her pocket. "Just in case," she explained, "Baby Browning, twenty-five ACP. I've always heard it was the best pocket gun." She explained with a grin, "It doesn't have a forward sight, so when someone with a real gun takes it away from you, he can shove it up your ass easier." With that, we stepped over Lennie, and half carried Bric up the stairs. We stopped to let him rest for a few minutes in the lounge, while Mallory washed off some of the dried blood, found a tee shirt and flip-flops in a closet, and got a bottle of water out of the fridge.

Looking Dad over from head to foot, I came to a decision. "No cab driver in his right mind will ever pick us up. Let me call Billy for a ride." I reached for my phone and before I punched his number it chirped. The caller ID told me it was Bric's phone. I hit the speaker so we could all hear. I didn't know how to answer, since we had their hostage, so I just cut to the chase again. "Get your money, assholes?"

The answer almost dripped with hate. "Your father is a dead man," he started. "How did you think we would let him go when you fill two suitcases full of shredded newspapers?" Before I could answer, Bric grabbed my phone. He almost shouted into the receiver. "Dead man? I'll show you a dead man! Listen motherfuckers. I'm standing in this piece of shit you call a boat. I just watched your boss meet his maker. I'll wait here so you can join him in Hell!"

Before I could caution my father that he was in no condition to meet four kidnappers, probably all with guns, we heard a soft popping sound, one, two, three, four, over the phone, and then it went dead.

"What was that?" I asked.

"I've heard that sound over the phone before, long ago," Mallory answered. "I think that was popping was the sound of a low caliber suppressed gun, what you call a silencer." She added with a smile, "They only make a 'zip!' sound in James Bond movies." A moment later I recognized Billy's satphone number on my cell.

"Billy?"

169

"Hi Brody," came the soft but confident answer on the other end. "I'm sorry, I'm afraid I just shot your father's phone and his car. I fear that neither are usable anymore."

"Are you okay?" Mallory asked.

"Oh, everyone on this end is just fine, that is if you don't count the kidnappers." He hesitated for a moment, "They won't be bothering you anymore. Fortunately, my boss's clean-up crew is still in town. Mr. Wahl, are you there?"

"Bright-eyed and bushy-tailed, if you don't count a few piddly little bruises."

"Bruises?" I said, looking my father up and down. "Dad, you look like you have been run over by a herd of buffalo."

"Bric," Billy continued, "I'd like to request that you stay away from your apartment and garage for a day or so until we get the place tidied up a little more. I'll be there in a little while to pick you up."

I was curious, "So those bags were full of shredded newspaper? There never was a million dollars?"

Billy answered slowly, but you could tell he expected my question. "That's a good question. Ah, Mr. Goodman was sure that giving these goons a million dollars would not have affected your father's safe recovery. He was also confident, I could either arrange for his safe release or," he paused. I could tell he was trying to be sensitive. "It was already too late."

I realized there was another problem.

"Billy, one more thing," I said, trying to be as tactful as possible. "After they are done at the apartment, they need to drop by here, preferably after dark," I explained that Lennie had unexpectedly run into us and suffered a small accident. I heard Billy chuckle a little. "I better get my associates out of town pretty soon." He said, "Or they are going to need a bigger truck."

With that, he hung up.

Dad shuddered, then growled. "I'll never set foot in that place again. Let Kevin know that he can rent it out to the staff, or just take it over himself."

Understanding Dad's reluctance, something was eating me that I had to ask. "Uh, this might not be the best time, but exactly what happened to Luis and Jose?"

I could tell Bric was still a little uncomfortable thinking about what happened. "Like I told you before, they invited me up to the apartment for a drink after the parade. We got outside of a decent portion of my tequila and rum. I started thinking about flaking out on my couch. Suddenly, someone put a pillowcase over my head, pulled my hands behind me, and put a rope around my waist. I jumped up, pulled the bag off my head, and started to fight." He smiled grimly. "I guess they thought two Mexicans could subdue one old man. Needless to say, it didn't go as they planned. I nuked the bastards! I didn't understand why I got attacked, and I was standing with my back to the door trying to figure out what to do with the meat, and somebody cracked me from behind." He gingerly touched the back of his head. "I woke up hogtied to that chair. I was pretty sure it was Lennie's so-called playroom on the *Bucks Up*. I guess I was right. From what little Russian I know, they paid Luis and Jose to help me get captured."

"Mallory," I said, changing the subject. "was that popping sound what you thought it was?"

"Billy sort of let you know," she answered. "When he apologized for killing your dad's phone and car." This time she smiled a little. "Billy admitted he does more for Mr. Goodman than just fly him around."

I gave a low whistle. "I'll say he does."

We took Dad home to the houseboat. Mallory, the nurse looked him over, checked his vitals, patched the open wounds, and pronounced, "It's all too far from his heart to kill him. He may have a mild concussion." She kissed him tenderly on the forehead. "Get a few days' rest, heal up and you'll be good as new."

"Heal up?" Bric growled. "I haven't had a thing to eat since Saturday, and other than that bottler of water you gave me, which I consider only good for a mixer, I haven't had a drink since our so-called friends tried to kidnap me." He stood up, pulled on one of my clean shirts, and announced. "Let's go to lunch!"

Mallory and I stood too. "I'm a bit peckish myself," Mallory added, using a term she learned in England. "We bought food, but never got around to eating it." She looked at me, "Where to?"

I couldn't help but laugh. "Back to Hogfish!"

It seemed like days since we occupied that waterside table at the Hogfish Bar and Grill, but looking at my watch, it had only been a few hours. The same server was still in charge of that table. When she saw who it was, she threw the menus on the table with disgust. "You again? Why don't you just save some time for both of us, drop a couple of twenties on the table, and leave without ordering?" I assured her that we planned to stay and eat this time. Mal and I ordered bottled water, but Bric had some catching up to do. "Code Rum and Coke. Make it a double" he ordered. The server looked closer at my dad's bandages, bruises, and scrapes. "What happened to you, Bric? Get run over by a train?"

"You oughta see the other guys," he answered smugly.

He never misses a beat.

Southernmost Son

Wayne Gales

21

Bric's recovery was almost miraculous. It was only a week later that he reminded me. "It's time for that party. We promised Becky and Brenda a proper bash when we got back from Mexico. Tell them to let everyone know." Mallory and I had like two days to clean up the yacht, arrange food and drink, and hang enough lights to keep some drunk from falling down the stairs and into the cabin. The invite list looked like a Who's Who of Key West's GLTBQ community. I was glad we were berthed at the marina so the crowd could spill out on the dock and not sink the *Seaglass* in Birkenstocks and white zinfandel.

Growing up, I lived with my mother in Sandusky, when my mom and dad divorced. When I came back to Key West to live with my father, I was so homophobic I would eat a banana sideways, like an ear of corn. After he got the houseboat and I met Scarlett and all of Dad's gay and lesbian friends, I grew to know they were some of the kindest, gentlest people in the world, had no intention of trying to 'convert' me, and proved to be some of Bric's hardest working and most loyal employees when he had the Bed and Breakfast, and later on Hunks. Tonight, the *Seaglass* was awash with gay, lesbian, and every other orientation imaginable. I understand now a conversation I had a long time ago when a relative explained to me that you could not define the world with just two sexes, man and woman. Comfortable in the environment, Mallory and I danced indiscriminately with whoever asked throughout the night.

While the function was in full swing and Bric was well oiled with rum with no eligible targets in sight, I figured the timing was right to broach the question.

I put an arm around his shoulder and led him to a quiet part of the boat. "Dad, this is crazy. You're living in an old single-wide that's seen its better day on Geiger Key and I'm in a tiny houseboat in Garrison Bight. We've got enough money to buy the biggest house on Shark Key. I think it's time for us to find a decent place and move you in with us."

That suggestion went over like a lead balloon. "I like my little place, and it's barely broken in," he answered with a

175

snort. "It's on a deep-water canal, and my flats boat is always ready to go on a whim. Besides," he added, "I've had my fill of crowds, noisy music, and pasty-white cruise tourists."

It was time to put my foot down. With Mallory by my side for moral support, I made a stand. "We don't want you up there by yourself. We'll find a family home for you, me, Mal, and your grandchild." As firmly as I could, I stressed, "That's final." I thought for a second and added. "We would be fine with a place up the keys, away from crowds. We can start looking tomorrow. *Capiche?*"

He could tell when 'no' wasn't going to be an acceptable answer. He brightened for a moment and answered. "How about a four-bedroom luxury condo with a nice kitchen, two baths, and an incredible sea view?"

I was relieved he was coming around but wandered about where this place was. "Exactly." I asked, "Where is this wonderful condo?"

With a smile, Bric opened his arms wide and bowed with a sweeping gesture, "Welcome to your new home, at least until your rug rat can get around good enough to fall overboard."

I looked at Mallory with wide eyes. She had caught on quicker than I did and nodded in agreement. "*Seaglass* it is," patting her growing tummy, "with the understanding we are firmly planted on terra firma before this urchin begins to crawl." Bricsmiled, shook my hand to confirm his agreement, then gave Mallory and me a warm embrace to seal the deal. "Just think, we can change our view every day if we want. What could possibly be better?"

With the uncomfortable part of the night out of our way, we went back to our friends. I could tell that Bric while enjoying the booze, was getting a little bored with the crowd. The great bunch of people did not exactly create a target-rich environment for his favorite pastime, namely chasing women. By eleven, I could see him getting antsy, and he started looking for a tactful exit. Finding me in the crowd, he tossed his last drink, put a hand on my shoulder, and said. "Son, do you mind holding down the fort for the rest of the party? I hear a barstool on Duval Street calling my name." Looking around, he confessed, "Wonderful party, but I'm starting to get nookie withdrawal symptoms." I smiled but groaned inwardly. It wasn't the first time my dad left me holding the bag.

Or the last.

Before I could answer, and almost on cue, a pair of soft hands reached from behind and covered his eyes.

"What, and leave me to drink your booze by myself? Don't you dare leave me with all these pretty girls, I might jump the fence again." Dad recognized the voice and turned around, smiling. "My rescuer! Karen, why did it take you so long to get here!" With an arm around her, he turned back to me, still grinning. "Son, mind taking over? Ah, I see two barstools in our future now." I couldn't help but laugh. He was determined to bail, and now he had a willing accomplice. With a shooing, motion I told them, "Go on you lovebirds. Dad, I'll see you in the morning so we can work out moving arrangements." I sent them off, wondering if bad judgment and sufficient alcohol would make him pop the question again.

This time, he might be surprised with the answer.

Before they could start down the gangplank, an ominous-looking black Ford Expedition pulled up on the street leading to the dock. I saw my father tense up, looking for a place to dive, half expecting someone to open the door with guns blazing. Instead, a man in a three-piece pin-striped suit and a fedora got out of the back seat with a briefcase, walked up to the ramp, and announced, "I have a letter for Mallory Wahl." He walked past Bric and Karen without a glance. Looking up at me with a relieved look, Dad commented. "Who's gonna show up next, Jimmy Hoffa?"

"Who?" I asked.

"Never mind," he answered and they walked down the ramp, around the SUV, and into the night.

Mal heard her name and approached the suit. "I'm Mallory," she said. The suit popped the latches on the briefcase and handed Mal the letter. You have a message from Mr. Goodman. He tipped his hat in greeting, turned, and walked away.

With a puzzled expression, she sat on a nearby chair, opened the envelope, and read it without expression. I figured whatever it said was a private manner, none of my business, and left her alone while I mingled. A few minutes later she found me and said softly, patting her growing baby bump, "Brody, I'm a little tired. Would you mind if I went back to the houseboat? After the party, you can bum a ride home, or just stay here, and I can pick you up in the morning." I gave her a kiss and handed her the Jeep keys. Before she left, she gave me a fierce hug and pressed the letter into my hands. Worried about what was in the letter, I retreated to a quiet corner, sat down under a light, and opened it. The first thing I noticed it was written two weeks ago.

My dearest Mallory. Words can't describe how excited your grandparents are at expecting their great-grandchild. I certainly hope they get to see him or her before they join me in Shamayim, what Brody calls Heaven. Yes, my goddaughter, if you are reading this, I have left this tired old body to continue my adventure, hopefully not in Gehenna, Hell, although I probably deserve that fate. Please shed no tears, but rejoice. I have lived a full life, over nine decades, and there's no reason to mourn. As I told you at the wedding, your child, or children should you choose to have more, will be well provided for with a college education of their choice, and a trust fund when they turn twenty-five. I love your husband and Brody is a good man, but a good education is more valuable than all the treasure on earth. I'm confident you will ensure that college is part of their future.

I close this letter to tell you that Moishe, Golda, and I love you beyond description. I've enclosed a small token of my love. I understand that you and Brody live comfortably. Perhaps this can be used to do mankind good and compensate for some of the regrettable deeds I have committed.

Yours forever,

It was signed with an unreadable scribble, written by a feeble hand. I looked in the envelope and pulled out a check.

I've never seen so many zeros.

With a tear in my eye, thinking about the thoughts my love must be going through, I shoved the letter in a back pocket and went back to the crowd. I tried to be a pleasant host for the rest of the evening, but all I wanted to do was run home and hold my bride.

Southernmost Son

Wayne Gales

Epilogue

The *Seaglass* rode peacefully above us in the gentle sea a few hundred yards off Boca Grande Key, a place dear to Bric's heart. Lounging on an inflatable rubber ducky, he plucked another boiled Key West Pink Shrimp off the floating table, dipped it in cocktail sauce, and tossed the tail over his shoulder to a waiting crowd of grunts, snappers, and needlefish. He took a long pull from his drink and motioned with the Solo cup toward the nearby low island, covered with just a few bushes and scrub pine. I think his eyes got a little misty, "That's where this whole adventure started. If I hadn't found that wreck, those lead bars, and all that gold, I would be chasing strange skirts and ended my days in a rocking chair at some assisted living community in Boca Raton, eating baby food for dinner."

"I think it's more likely you'll die by breaking your neck after falling naked out of somebody's second-floor window at ninety-two."

My thoughts turned serious.

"Then I would have never met Mallory, we wouldn't have found all that treasure, and," I swept my arms around the yacht. "We would have never sailed this little tub halfway around the world."

"Oh," Dad corrected me, "Moishe would have still found us in Key West, we would have probably still gone to Haiti, and," motioning toward Mallory. "You would have still met the love of your life."

Changing the subject, I brought up something that had just entered my mind.

"Speaking of love, did you ever pop the question to Karen again? I had a distinct impression her answer this time might have surprised you."

Dad, leaned his head back for a moment, letting the tropical water give his hat a cooling drench. "I didn't ask her, *she* asked *me*. Or at least she hinted she would like me to ask her again. After taking advantage of the, er, moment, I kissed her tenderly and told her, 'Marriage is a young man's folly and an old man's comfort' but this man was too old. As she once told me a long time ago, there was just too much water under that bridge." He sighed as if he might have made the wrong decision. "We parted friends, but I doubt I'll ever see her again."

Mallory, happy to have her figure back, lounged nearby on an inflatable raft, topless, wearing only a tiny bikini bottom, interrupted our conversation. She had already adopted *my* dad as *her* dad.

"Father, you can't be alone for the rest of your life. That's just not you."

I could almost see his merry eyes behind his mirror-lensed Costas.

"Oh, nobody ever said I would be alone. Even at my age, life is indeed too short."

I heard a noise on board *Seaglass*, and then the air filled with the wails of a hungry eight-month-old. Mallory rolled off her float and paddled toward the ladder. "It sounds like Brody Junior needs a tit to suck on."

"A man after my own taste," I quipped. Before Mal gracefully climbed up the ladder, she sent a spray of seawater my way with a hand, soaking my chips and contaminating my ice water. In a moment, the crying stopped, no doubt muffled by one of those perfect breasts. Fifteen minutes later, she walked to the rail and handed down little Russell Broderick Wahl, naked, well-fed, and happy. I gave him a salty kiss then threw him in the water where he swam fifteen feet to Grandpa, all underwater.

That boy is gonna make me look like a landlubber when he grows up.

Mallory came back to the side of the boat. "Since your hands are free now, you can have his twin sister, too."

"Come here, Abby." I reached up while she reached down for my arms with a big smile. Brody was going to be a fish; Abigail Elizabeth was going to be an angel.

There was both a comfort and a fear that the twins had a paid college education and a hefty trust fund in their future. And there was that check from Goodman. I don't know what plans Mallory had for that money, but I have no doubt it will be spent to better the world.

I still remember those days when I was a teenager on a derelict cabin cruiser in the middle of Florida Bay. Back then, I couldn't afford expensive tennis shoes, fancy computers, or even an occasional Big Mac. But I still look at those days as the happiest of my life. What can be more valuable in life than having no more than a roof over your head, a good mask a sharp speargun, starry skies at night, and a father that loved you beyond description?

What will they become?

We shall see.

Also Available on Amazon By Wayne Gales in Kindle, Paperback and Audible

Treasure Key
Key West Normal
Nobody's Inn Key West
Key West Normal
Everybody's Bar in Key West
Southernmost Exposure
Bone Island Bodies
Once Upon a time in Key West
Living and Dying in Key West Time
The last three books available on Audible as a Trilogy
Texas in The Tropics

Cooking for the Hearing Impaired

Children's books, Illustrated by Lori Kus

We Wish to Fish
Sun, Sand, and the Salty Sea
Caught No Fish

Made in United States
Orlando, FL
07 June 2025

61917868R00105